Defending Zoe

D1713779

Stone Knight's MC
Book 9

Megan Fall

Defending Zoe
Published by Megan Fall

This book is a work of fiction. Any
similarities to real people,
places, or events are not intentional and are
purely
the result of coincidence. The characters,
places, and events
in this story are fictional.

Copyright © 2020 by Megan Fall. All rights
reserved

All rights reserved. This publication may not
be reproduced,
distributed, or transmitted in any form
without the express
written consent of the author except for the
use of small quotes or excerpts used in book
reviews.

Dedication

To my grandmother

Your love and support means the world to me.
Thank you so much for all you have done for me!

Contents

Chapter One
Dagger

Dagger snarled as he found himself locked in his room again. He sat on the floor and breathed in the quiet for a few minutes. The club was expanding a lot, and most of his brothers now had their own women. Things were changing, and he knew it was for the better, he just didn't know if he would ever find the same thing.

Only a handful of brothers knew he was a marine. He liked to keep that part of his life private. They had stationed him in Afghanistan with his best friend Ty. They grew up together and were as thick as thieves. When Ty became a marine, Dagger followed. A month before they were finished their tour, the vehicle they were in got taken out by a roadside bomb. Dagger hadn't even gotten a scratch, but Ty had been killed.

Dagger had been lost for a long time, suffering, and not knowing where to turn. Then one day Preacher walked into his life and saved him. He had found a home with The Stone Knight's and had slowly healed. He learned to laugh again and had gained a ton of new brothers.

Now he was known as the comedian of the club. He went out of his way to make sure he kept things light. He could forget when things were crazy, and the brothers were laughing. It helped keep him sane.

But when it was quiet, like it was now, Dagger savoured it. Sometimes he wanted to just breathe and remember Ty. He always complained when they pulled this shit, but secretly he sometimes needed it.

Figuring he had been in the room long enough, he climbed to his feet and walked into the bathroom. He grabbed the nearest towel, wrapped it around his arm, and walked over to the bedroom window. With little effort, he pulled back and slammed his elbow into the glass. It shattered immediately, and he efficiently pulled the leftover shards out of the way. When the frame was clean, he dropped the towel over the sill and climbed out.

In minutes he was walking in the main doors. Dragon noticed him first, and his head spun from him to the back hall, and to him again.

"I thought you were in your room?" Dragon frowned. "Where the hell did you come from?"

Dagger just grinned. "I have dynamite you idiots. You know you can't hold me down for long." He sat at the bar and motioned for Smoke to grab him a shot of whiskey.

"If you blew a hole through the goddamned wall, I will rip you a new asshole," Preacher growled as he sat down beside him.

Dagger smirked at his president. "I'd never do that," he lied in mock horror. "Besides, I have a date with a hottie. I can't break her heart by not showing up."

"Who's it this time?" Dragon questioned. "The clerk at the convenience store, the bartender, or one of the dancers at the strip club?"

"They had their chance," Dagger smirked with a wave of his hand. "This is a new girl I've been seeing for about a month now."

"You going to bring her around so we can meet her?" Trike asked as he joined them.

"Nah," Dagger denied. "It's just a girl I'm having some fun with."

"You'll find the right one soon," Trike smirked. "And I bet she's going be a handful."

"Right," Steele added. "I want to see you with someone who gives you a run for your money."

Dagger chuckled. "Not likely," he told them. "My girls going to be sweet, soft, and quiet." All the bikers within hearing distance snorted.

"Your girls going to be a hell raiser," Sniper snickered. "I bet you one hundred dollars she's worse than you," he challenged, as he slapped a hundred-dollar bill on the bar. Immediately six more hundreds landed on top of the first one.

"You fuckers suck," Dagger complained. "I'll take that bet, and you can all kiss my ass when I prove you wrong."

"You're going to have to sell your Harley to come up with the money you'll owe us all," Steele teased.

"Fucking bikers," Dagger growled as he pushed off his stool and made his way to the door. As he opened it he heard the bikers laughter following him.

It wouldn't happen, he thought to himself. His sweet girl was out there, and he'd fucking find her.

Chapter Two
Zoe

Zoe stood at the side of the country road, hiding in the cover of the trees. It was well past midnight, pitch black out, and she was practically invisible in her dark clothing. She pulled the hood up on the sweatshirt she was wearing, hoping it would hide the long red hair she had hidden underneath it.

Zoe was just outside of The Stone Knight's compound, and she was trembling with nerves. She had positioned herself halfway between the main gate, and the gate she had found out Mario and his men used. She wanted to make sure she was able to see both. Right now, she was just studying the compound and looking for weaknesses. Unfortunately, there weren't many, and that made her nervous.

Six months ago, she had been so happy. She had been away at college and loving her time there. She had a ton of friends, but her best friend had been her older sister Amber. Sadly, her parents had died when she was fifteen, and Amber was eighteen. Amber had dropped out of college and gotten a job, so she could look after her.

Things were great until Amber had been killed. Zoe had still been at college at the time, but she had been visited by two detectives that had delivered the news. Charles and Candace had been an odd-looking pair. Charles was overweight and older, while Candace had wore a ton of makeup and been younger. But Zoe hadn't cared what they looked like, it had been what they said that broke her.

Her poor sister had been working as a bartender for Mario. Mario apparently was a mob boss of sorts, that was affiliated with The Stone Knight's motorcycle club. From what the detectives told her, Amber had seen something she shouldn't have, and the men had killed her because of it. They had found her poor sister strangled in her apartment.

The news had devastated Zoe. She had left college, sold everything she could, and come to Haven. She had stood at the gravesite alone as they had laid her sister to rest. She didn't tell a soul, wanting the time to herself. Plus, she didn't want anyone to know she was there.

When Zoe had asked if they had charged the club or Mario, the detectives had told her they hadn't. Apparently the two detectives in charge of the case, Darren and Colin, were crooked. They had messed with the evidence and conveniently lost all the proof. There was nothing anyone could do.

Zoe had sat in her sisters apartment for a week solid after the burial and cried. Then she had sold the place and gotten something smaller. The cost of the funeral had taken most of her savings, and Amber had been paying her college costs, so she hadn't had much saved up either.

One day she had woken up angry and pissed at the world. Her sister had been killed, and nobody seemed to be doing anything about it. Zoe wasn't a violent person, but she figured it was time to become one. If no one else would take action against the club, she would.

Zoe had spend days coming up with different ways she could get back at the club and Mario. Then she had started gathering information on the members and the compound. She had studied everything and come up with several ideas she planned to put into action. When she was done, the club and mobster would be begging to turn themselves in.

Zoe smiled then, as she spun on her heals and jogged down the road. She had parked her tiny beat up car far down the road, and she was anxious to get back to it. She would head to her apartment, get some sleep, and then put things into motion.

Zoe reached her car and climbed inside. Before she started it up, she stared at her sisters picture that she had taped to the dash.

"I will make this right," she told the photo. "Those men will pay, and they will never know what hit them."

For the first time in a long time, she found herself excited about something. She couldn't wait to get things started, and she couldn't wait to see the reactions of the tough, badass bikers, when she rained hell on them, Zoe style.

Things were about to get extremely interesting.

Chapter 3
Dagger

Dagger sauntered back into the clubhouse the next morning, grinning after his date. It had gone well, but Dagger knew it was time to end it. The girl was great, but she wasn't long term. She was getting clingy, and she was pushing for their relationship to move onto the next level.

He noticed Steele, Tripp, Sniper and Raid sitting at a table, and approached. As soon as he was seated, Navaho placed a hot plate of eggs, bacon and toast in front of him. He nodded his thanks and dug in.

"I assume by the fucking grin, you had a good night?" Sniper asked.

Dagger stopped eating to address the brother. "Fucking awesome," he confirmed.

"So, you bringing her into the club?" Raid questioned.

"Nope," Dagger replied. "I'm ending it."

"But you just said it was awesome," Raid grunted with a shake of his head.

"Yep, but she's getting fucking clingy," he complained as he set down his fork.

"How so?" Steele pushed.

"She wants to move in here and she wants a vest," he admitted. "We've been dating for a month," he said in exasperation. "I don't mind seeing her once in a while and hanging out, but she's not girlfriend material."

"What's she look like?" Sniper asked.

Dagger grinned. "Fucking tall, long hair, fake tits, she's perfect. Just like a Barbie."

"And that's bad?" Raid grinned.

"I want real," Dagger huffed. "If I ever settle down, I want the exact opposite of Lisa. I want someone small, someone I can protect. And she better have whatever god gave her. Fake tits look good, but they feel like shit." He stopped talking when Tripp looked like he would tear someone's head off.

"What the fucks the matter with you?" Dagger questioned.

Tripp growled, and Dagger got a bad feeling in his gut. "You're dating Lisa?"

"I said that already," Dagger sighed in frustration. "You got to keep up brother." The brothers all chuckled, but Tripp just glared at him.

"Before I got back with gypsy, I dated Lisa," Tripp reluctantly explained. Dagger's back went straight and he could feel the tension at the table mount. "She was a good time, but just like with you, she got clingy. Lisa expected a vest and wasn't happy she didn't get one."

"She cause you any trouble?" Steele asked.

"No, but then it appears that she just moved on to another brother," he growled. Dagger pushed back his chair and headed for the door.

"Where the fuck you going?" Sniper questioned.

"To fucking give her a piece of my mind," Dagger growled back. "And spread the word about her. I don't want her pulling this shit again."

In minutes, he was back on his Harley and headed out the gates. It took him fifteen minutes to get back to Lisa's. He pulled up to her house, climbed off, and headed to the door. He didn't even make it all the way, before she threw it open and raced towards him in a fucking skimpy robe.

"Dagger honey, you missed me," she cried, as she threw herself at him. He pried her off him and stepped back. She immediately placed her hands on her hips and looked up at him.

"What's your problem?" she purred. "We can move this inside if your uncomfortable."

"Not fucking going inside," he growled. "You were with Tripp?" he asked.

She lost her soft expression and sneered at him.

"You bringing up my history?" she complained. "Tripp isn't here, you are."

"Yeah, only because he dumped your ass when he saw Fable again," he returned.

"He wasn't right for me," she pouted. "It never would have worked. You're the one I really want," she soothed, back to being sweet.

"So, it had nothing to do with him not giving you a vest?" he questioned.

Again, she lost her smile. "I worked hard for that vest," she yelled.

"Jesus," Dagger huffed, throwing up his hands. "Your mood swings are giving me whiplash."

"We're good together," she tried again. "Your way sexier than Tripp was."

Dagger grinned at her. "I am," he agreed. "We're done though," he announced as he turned back to his bike.

"What?" she screeched. "I'm not going through this shit again. Your giving me that vest."

Dagger climbed on his Harley and started it up. "Not happening," he yelled back at her, as he pulled away. "And I've put out word for the brothers to stay clear of you."

Dagger roared down the road, but her screams followed him. He ignored her and headed home, but he had a feeling she was a little unhinged. He'd have to keep an eye out for her, he thought. The club didn't need anymore trouble.

Chapter 4
Zoe

Zoe was casing the strip club today. She didn't dare go inside, so she was sitting across the street at a donut shop. She had her laptop out, and was trying to dig stuff up on the club as she watched for any of the bikers or Mario to appear. So far it had been mostly dancers, and a couple big guys she figured were bouncers.

She'd had so many bottles of apple juice, she hoped she hadn't missed anyone on one of her many trips to the bathroom. She hated coffee though, along with most hot drinks, and always drank apple juice when she was nervous. Now it was coming back to bite her in the ass. She wiggled on the seat, as she felt the need to go again creeping up on her.

Suddenly, a slick black car pulled into the lot. She hit the glass window in her haste to get closer and cursed her stupidity. Moving back slightly, she watched as the driver's door opened and Mario stepped out. She'd seen pictures of him, but she hadn't had the chance to see him in person yet.

He was stunning, wearing dress shoes, jeans, a crisp white shirt, and a suit jacket. His hair was thick, black, and slightly messy, and his face was to die for. Unfortunately, he scared the absolute shit out of her. He just had a look about him that promised violence. She watched as he scanned the surrounding area, and she had to fight the urge to drop to the floor and hide.

How the hell was she supposed to get back at him for murdering her sister? Zoe wouldn't stand a chance against him. She watched him as he turned and strode into the club. She had several ideas of things she could do to the bikers, but she had no idea what to do to him.

Zoe watched for another twenty minutes, but no one else showed up except for Mario's partner in the club, Nick. She had researched him as well, so she knew what he looked like. Fortunately, he wasn't on her hit list, so he was in the clear.

Zoe snapped her laptop shut, headed to the bathroom one more time, then left. Opening her car door, she threw her laptop in the back, and headed to the hardware store. The first thing she did was grab a cart, the things she needed were heavy, and she knew she'd never get them to her car without it.

She headed straight to the paint section and ordered six cans of pink paint. When the man asked her what shade she was looking for, she told him she didn't care, as long as it was bright. While he was mixing it, she looked at brushes and paint trays.

"Ahem," the man that had helped her coughed, as he cleared his throat to get her attention. She turned to see what he wanted.

"This is a lot of paint. You can roll it on, but it's going to take you a while. Cheap paint sprayers are on sale this week, and even if you use it only one time, it's worth it," he explained.

She chewed on her bottom lip, as she considered what he said. Zoe didn't have a lot of extra money to spare, but she wanted to get it done as quickly as possible. She didn't want to get caught either, so that was a big reason why she nodded and let him show her the sprayer.

Fifteen minutes later, she pushed the cart out the door, and headed to her car. Her head was down as she tried to pull her keys out of her pocket. Suddenly, she smacked into something, and the cart stopped. She shoved it harder, but it wouldn't budge.

"You push that any harder into me and it's going to leave a mark," a man declared as he chuckled.

Her head snapped up, and she found herself staring at the most beautiful man she'd ever seen. She smiled at him and started to apologize, until she noticed the biker vest he was wearing. Immediately she knew he belonged to the biker club that killed her sister.

"Excuse me," Zoe apologized as she pushed the cart around him and lost her smile.

He frowned, obviously curious about her sudden mood change. "You need some help with all that?" he questioned.

"Nope," she denied as she glared at him. Then she noticed his name patch. "I don't take help from bikers Dagger," she told him. He didn't seem phased by her attitude, and his smile got bigger.

"Even good looking ones?" he teased. And then he winked.

Zoe stared at him as her heart stuttered. "You're dangerous," she declared, as she willed herself to look away. "Have a nice day," she called as she practically ran to her car.

She didn't know what had just happened, but she had a feeling he could very well end up being a problem.

Chapter 5
Dagger

Dagger watched the girl practically run away from him with her cart. That was probably a first for him. Usually girls were all over him. She had almost seemed frightened of him though, and he didn't like that at all. He kept an eye on her as she loaded several bags in the trunk of a shit car, and pushed the cart to the cart return.

Her hair was like nothing he had ever seen. It was a stunning red colour, and when the sun hit it, it seemed to glow. When she looked up, he found himself looking into the face of an angel. His heart literally stopped when she smiled at him. But then she seemed to shut down, and that's when the fear had kicked it.

Dagger wondered if it was because he was a biker. Some people thought all bikers were one percenters, and just out to raise hell. Maybe she had met a biker like that before, and her image of all bikers was now clouded. Whatever it was, he was determined to find her again, because she intrigued him.

He drove back to the clubhouse and headed straight to the garage. Jude and Wrench were restoring an old mustang, and he wanted to see how they were doing. He found them in the back bay, fiddling with something under the hood. Jude had painted the car a beautiful metallic blue, and it looked phenomenal. The man was a genius.

"Looking good boys," Dagger called when he was close. Both men popped their heads up and grinned at him.

"You meant the car right, and not our asses?" Jude chuckled. Then he peered around at his own. "Although mine looks good. My Little Rainbow tells me all the time."

Wrench rolled his eyes. "Here we go again with the ego. And don't bring my sister up when your talking about your ass," he snarled.

Dagger laughed as he dragged out a bench and took a seat. "You do impressive work," he complimented the brothers.

"It's all Jude," Wrench declared. "I just hand him parts."

"I love doing this," Jude replied. "If I could, I'd open a garage next to this one, that just restored old cars. But I'm the only one that knows anything about them."

"There's a guy in the next town that I hear does the same thing. He's some rich boy. His parents want him to go into politics like them, but he's bought an old run-down farm house and he works on old cars in his barn. I hear he's just as good as you," Dagger imparted.

Jude's interest was hard to miss. "I'll hunt him down and have a word. Thanks."

Dagger nodded, then he asked what he wanted to know. "What did it feel like when you met your one?"

Jude grinned at him. "Like I'd been hit over the head with a hammer. I knew right away, but I fought the pull for a while. I honestly wasn't planning on settling down. You can see how that worked out for me."

"You think you found yours?" Wrench asked curiously.

"A girl ran into me with a shopping cart at the hardware store," Dagger admitted.

Jude started chuckling. "November did the exact same thing to me. You may have another klutz on your hands. Word of advice. Stay away from paint, trees, shower curtains, cooking spray, you name it. She'll turn it into a weapon of destruction."

Dagger smirked. "Your girls certainly a nut. But my girl was just distracted. The part I don't like though, is that when she saw my vest she seemed to get scared."

Wrench moved away from the car and crossed his arms. "She could be in trouble somehow, other than that, she had a bad experience with a biker."

"That's what I was thinking," Dagger agreed. "I need to find her and set her straight."

"You may freak her out more if you follow her everywhere," Wrench warned. "You need to be careful."

Dagger sagged, he certainly didn't want to make the situation worse. "Any suggestions?" he inquired.

"Just take your time," Jude advised. "My Rainbow was on the run, and standoffish when I met her. Just keep at it. Show her your only there to help and you'll slowly gain her trust."

"Right," Dagger nodded. "Appreciated." Then he turned and walked away.

"Twenty bucks says she shoots him," he heard Wrench say just before he was out of hearing distance.

Chapter 6
Zoe

Zoe waited until two in the morning before heading out to the compound. She had visited a thrift store earlier in the day and purchased a boy's bike and wagon for twenty-five dollars. She wanted the bikers to think it was a kid if they caught her on cameras. The wagon was now full of paint and the sprayer, and she was almost to the compound. She would have taken her car, but she'd seen the cameras when she'd scoped it earlier, and she didn't want them to trace her plates.

It was a beautiful night, so Zoe enjoyed the ride there. The last couple months had taken a toll on her, both physically and mentally. She had tried several times to get a hold of the two detectives again, but they weren't calling her back. She hoped they were just busy with other cases.

When she reached the compound, she slowed and pulled her bike into the cover of the trees. Zoe had on a pair of black runners, black sweatpants, black gloves and a black hoodie. She had her hair pulled back in a tight bun. She knew she had to be extremely careful with it, because of the colour. It wouldn't be hard for the bikers to find her. She'd also pulled on a baseball cap to shield her face more.

Zoe pulled two cans of paint out of the wagon and carried them to the gate. She was really hoping that because of how late it was, and how dark it was out, that the guard wouldn't notice her. She moved quickly as she attached the sprayer. It had a hand pump, so she didn't need power to work it, and it would be extremely quiet. In minutes she was applying the paint to the compound gates.

It took her twenty minutes to complete, and no one caught her. She grinned at the way it glowed, even in the dark. It was the perfect shade of pink, and it looked absolutely ridiculous. She loved it. It took three cans of paint, and she still had three left. Packing up her supplies, she peddled down to the other gate that Mario used, and got started on that one.

Zoe was even more cautious here. Mario was only one man, but he scared her more than the bikers. She thought back to the biker she had met at the hardware store. He was handsome, and if he wasn't a biker, she would have been interested. He had an amazing smile, and he seemed really nice. She shook her head and continued painting. She had to forget about him. If he was a biker, he was bad news.

Zoe was surprised when she finished without any trouble. Although she was only painting the outside. She bet if she tried to climb them it would be a completely different outcome.

She quickly packed up her supplies, hopped back on her bike, and headed back to her apartment. She had rented a storage unit from the landlord, so she could hide the bike and wagon in there for a while. Later on she could just ditch them somewhere.

Zoe reached the storage shed and put everything inside, then made her way up to her apartment. In minutes she had stripped, and shoved all her clothes in a knapsack she kept hidden in the back of her small closet. She jumped in the shower and made sure she was clean of every trace of pink paint, then headed to bed.

Zoe had also paid the man at the hardware store a hundred dollars. She told him one of the bikers had pulled a prank on her and she was getting him back. She begged him not to tell on her if they came in asking who bought the paint. Of course, he had agreed and pocketed her money.

As Zoe lay there she thought of the bikers. She wished she could be there to see their reaction. She would have placed a small camera in the trees if she thought she could have got away with it, but she knew the bikers would have found it. She fell asleep with a grin on her face. Zoe couldn't wait to get up tomorrow and head to the donut shop for her apple juice. She really hoped the biker's gates would be the talk of the town.

Chapter 7
Dagger

Dagger moved into the common room early the next morning, to find the bikers extremely pissed off. They seemed to be arguing amongst themselves about something, and Dagger only caught parts of it.

"Just repaint them," Sniper yelled.

"You can't do that, the paint will just bleed through. You've seen the fucking colour of it," Raid argued back.

Then the girls were in their corner, and they were grinning and clapping.

"Why didn't we think of that?" November asked the other girls.

"I don't know," Tiffany frowned. "Do you think we can convince them to leave it like that?"

Dagger had no idea what was going on, so he turned to Dragon, who happened to be the closest.

"What the hell's happened?" he questioned curiously.

Dragon shook his head. "You have to see it to believe it. Head out to the gates. Most of the clubs out there, anyway."

Suddenly the girls surrounded him. "Come on Dagger," Fable encouraged. "We'll be happy to show you."

Dagger trailed after them, out the doors, and across the compound. It surprised him to see how many brothers were actually out there, but the gates were only open a bit, and everyone seemed to be on the outside. The girls moved through the opening and Dagger followed. When he turned to see what everyone was looking at, his jaw dropped. The gates were covered in bright pink flowers. It looked like the flowers were daisies.

"What the fuck?" was all he could get out.

"Isn't it beautiful?" November questioned happily.

"Fucking beautiful my ass. Lucifer get your woman inside before I show her what I think of her comment," Preacher growled. As Dagger watched, Lucifer hurried to pull his klutz back inside.

"That's the craziest thing I've ever seen," Dagger declared. "Someone definitely wants our attention."

"I think someone in this town may be crazier than you," Steele chuckled.

"Why the fuck would someone do this?" Dagger asked.

"I have no fucking idea," Preacher snarled. "Mario's gate looks the same. Thank fuck, because he's the ass that decided we needed gates that provided more security. It's easy to paint these metal ones, it wouldn't have been easy to paint the old ones."

"Yep, but that just means the fucker did this because they couldn't get inside," Mario growled as he and Trent joined them. "We could have ended up with pink bikes and cars."

Preacher growled again. "Messing with a bikers Harley is a death sentence."

"And maybe whoever did this knows that," Dragon pushed.

"You pull anything off the tapes?" Preacher questioned Trent.

"I did," Trent confirmed. "But there isn't much to go on. It looks like a kid rode up on a fucking bike, trailing a wagon. They used a pump sprayer, so it didn't make a fucking sound. They wore black from head to toe and seemed to know where the cameras where placed. Whoever it was moved quickly and efficiently, they were in and out in under an hour," Trent explained.

"So, we got nothing?" Preacher frowned.

"We got pink paint," Steele declared. "I'll head over to the hardware store and see if anyone's bought any recently. The bike's a boy's bike, and it looks like a kid in the video. Could be somebody paid him to do this."

"So, we have someplace to start," Preacher grunted as he turned to the bikers that were closest. "Anyone know someone with a grudge against us that would pull something like this?"

Dagger immediately hung his head. "I broke up with a girl a couple days ago. She didn't take it well. Apparently, she's looking to hook up with a biker, as she went after Tripp first, but I had no idea until he told me."

"Find her and have a word," Preacher ordered.

Then they watched as a car pulled up. Of course, it had to be Darren and Colin. They got out and instantly started laughing. When Darren pulled out a camera and started taking pictures, Preacher started growling again. Darren stopped and stared at him.

"Evidence," Darren announced.

"Fucking detectives," Preacher growled. Then he seemed to get more pissed when a car went by, and everyone inside was laughing.

"Get what you can and let me know if you find anything," Preacher ordered. "Dagger find your bitch and get this sorted. And get this fucking paint off." Then he stormed into the compound.

Dagger sighed. Here we go again, he thought.

Chapter 8
Zoe

Zoe woke up early the next morning refreshed, and excited to see if word had spread yet. She hurried through her shower and got dressed. Shoving a couple bills in her pocket, she hurried down to the coffee shop across from the strip club. She got a muffin and apple juice and chose a table near the window.

The coffee shop was packed, and it wasn't long before customers starting talking. She caught the word pink paint several times, and laughter always followed it. She also watched as people showed each other their phone screens, which Zoe hoped meant pictures of the gates were being shared.

Grinning, she couldn't be happier. Zoe now knew her plan had been perfect. She didn't want to hurt any of the bikers, she just wanted to mess with them a bit. She wanted vengeance for her sister, but she wasn't a violent person. This, she was achieving her way.

When a car pulled up, and two detectives stepped out, she recognized one of them right away. Darren had been partners with Tripp at the time of her sister's death, and Charles and Candace had explained how the club and Mario had him in their back pocket. She watched as he stepped into the donut shop with his new partner. Immediately, they were swarmed by customers.

"Darren, any leads on the compounds decorator?" one lady chuckled. As Zoe watched, the detective laughed back.

"Not yet honey, but we're working on it. The bikers are going through the tapes their cameras caught, and they're headed to the nearest hardware stores.

It shouldn't be long before we know something," he explained. "Could just be kids pulling a prank."

"Do you think this is a one-time thing?" another customer asked.

"God, I hope not," Darren replied. "It's been quiet around here for a while now."

The customers finally left them alone, so the detectives made their way to the counter, and picked up coffees. Once they left, Zoe breathed a sigh of relief. She hoped the guy at the hardware store didn't snitch on her, but it left her feeling uneasy. She had more stuff planned. She didn't want to stop just yet.

Zoe considered going back to the hardware store, but decided that wouldn't be a great idea. She stood and threw out her garbage, then made her way back outside. The detectives said it could have been kids playing a prank. She really liked that idea, and knew she had to come up with some ideas where she could use that.

Zoe headed down the street and turned when she heard motorcycles approaching. As she watched two approach, one slowed and headed straight for her. She looked around in fright, but she was beside a park. There was literally nowhere to hide. And of course, it would be the good looking biker that she had met the other day, that stopped beside her with a big smile.

"Firecracker," he smirked. "It's so nice to see you again. She immediately glared at him.

"Why are you calling me Firecracker?" Zoe demanded.

"You get all fired up when you see me," he explained as he chuckled. "Must be the red hair making you act that way."

She threw up her arms in annoyance. "You've seen me once."

"Yep, and you were definitely a Firecracker," Dagger chuckled. "Go out to dinner with me?" he asked, and his quick subject change threw her.

"No," Zoe stubbornly answered.

"Yes," he quickly returned, pulling a glare from her.

"I don't date bikers," Zoe told him for the second time.

"Why?" Dagger asked in curiosity. She noticed the second biker was waiting for her answer as well, and she shifted nervously.

"Bikers are scary guys," she whispered. "They hurt people and do bad things."

Both bikers looked angry, and she moved to step back. Dagger's hand shot out and wrapped lightly around her arm.

"A biker hurt you?" Dagger growled.

"Yes," Zoe whispered as her voice cracked. "But it was because of what they did to the only family I had left."

Dagger looked extremely concerned, and his angry expression instantly turned sad. She didn't want to see that, so she yanked her arm back and took off. But she still heard the words he shouted after her.

"Not all bikers are bad Firecracker," Dagger bellowed.

Chapter 9
Dagger

Dagger watched sadly as the girl ran from him. This was getting more complicated by the minute. He was worried by what she said. The biker she was talking about had hurt her last family member. He didn't know if it was a parent or a sibling, but he didn't like that she was now all alone. Of course, it made him understand why she was so skittish around him.

"You got your work cut out for you," Steele told him. "A biker did a real number on her. It may be best to cut your losses. She may never come around."

Dagger glared at his brother. "Would you give up if it was Cassie?" he shot back.

"Fuck no," Steele growled. "But this could backfire on you. That's girls freaked, it's going to be damned hard to show her you're not like that biker, and not freak her out."

"Goddammit," Dagger growled. "I'll fucking figure something out."

"Right," Steele replied. "Maybe you should just stop being a biker, you'd have a better shot at her."

Dagger turned to his brother with a grin. "You're a fucking genius," he told him.

Steele shook his head. "I'm not fucking asking. Let's go to the hardware store, then go question your psycho ex."

Dagger nodded as the two pulled out on the road again. There was no sign of his girl, but he figured she had to live close. She'd walked from somewhere, he'd just have to figure out where. He saw her car once, so he figured he could search for it later and get her plates. He could give them to Trent and see if he could figure who she was and what happened to her family.

When they reached the hardware store, both stepped inside and headed for the paint department. They decided to work together, as it seemed more intimidating, rather than splitting to do the things Preacher had ordered.

When they reached the counter, a kid that had to be eighteen was standing there. He instantly started to smirk when he saw them, and if Dagger didn't know better, the kid already knew about their gates.

"Can I help you?" he asked a little too smugly.

"Who did you sell the pink paint to?" Steele immediately growled. Dagger chuckled when the kid paled.

"I don't know what you're talking about," the kid outright lied.

"You ever hear about how we handle people who don't answer our questions?" Dagger grinned.

The boy actually gulped. "I heard your wife's parents place blew up with her ex inside," the kid stammered as he stared at Steele.

"It did," Steele agreed. "They never proved it was us though." Dagger grinned, knowing the whole town figured it was them.

"Who bought the paint?" Steele asked again with less patience.

"Ah man," the kid sighed. "I promised I wouldn't tell. You guys keep your promises, right?" he asked. "Don't make me break my word."

Dagger sighed, he didn't want to do that. "Where's the security tapes?" he questioned.

The kid looked relieved. "We don't keep tapes," he told them.

Steele pointed up. "You have cameras," he announced.

"Oh, those aren't hooked up to anything," the kid told them. "The owner just hung them up to make customers think he was watching them. He says he's not forking out the dough when they work fine like that."

"Did the customer pay at the front, or pay you?" Dagger growled.

The kid grinned. "The customer paid me."

Steele looked pissed, but he pushed off the counter and headed for the doors. Dagger trailed behind.

"I have a feeling that kid liked whoever bought the paint," Steele declared as he pushed out the doors.

"How do you figure that?" Dagger questioned.

"He was fucking blushing every time we brought up the customer. He only seemed scared for a minute, then he was grinning again when he figured out we wouldn't hurt him. We're looking for a girl," Steele replied as he climbed on his bike.

"Well, Lisa's definitely a girl," Dagger huffed as he started up his bike. "She'd make any kid blush."

Dagger pulled out and headed in the direction of his ex's, with Steele right behind him.

As soon as they pulled into her driveway, the door was flung open, and she was running towards him in some tiny ass shorts and a bikini top.

"Dagger darling," she cried as she flung herself at him and his bike. "I knew you'd change your mind."

He had no choice but to catch her, and she hit him like a ton of bricks. The bike rocked, but he managed to stop it from falling. Steele was chuckling beside him.

"Oh, this is going to be fun," the ass smirked.

Chapter 10
Dagger

Dagger immediately pried Lisa off him. As soon as she was free, he stepped away from the bike. He looked down to find her frowning up at him and glancing between him and Steele.

"You came back for me," she purred. "I knew you couldn't say goodbye."

"I'm not here because I want you back," Dagger growled. "I'm here because the club's gates were vandalized, and we need to know if you did it."

She immediately grinned. "I heard about that. I even got pics sent me."

"Did you do it?" Steele demanded. "The guy at the hardware store said it was a girl who bought the paint."

Suddenly Lisa threw up her arms and glared. "So, you assumed it was me? I'm with Dagger, why would I do anything to hurt him or the club?" she pouted.

"I'm not with you. I broke up with you a couple days ago," Dagger growled.

"You just need a break. We'll be together again soon," she declared as she smiled up at him.

Steele shook his head. "Bat shit crazy."

"Listen, I want nothing to do with you," Dagger insisted, but she was already shaking her head.

"I turned down Tripp for you," she proudly admitted. "We'll get past this. I made dinner. Can you stay?" Dagger blinked at her rapid subject change.

"And it's time to go," Steele frowned as he started backing out of her driveway.

Dagger completely agreed. He moved towards his bike and climbed on.

"Can I have a kiss before you go?" Lisa called, as he was hurrying to get his bike on the street.

"No," he yelled. Then he started it and roared out after Steele. They didn't talk the whole way back, and Dagger was thankful.

When they pulled up to the gates, Smoke and Wrench were painting them with a white primer.

"Even that looks better," Steele grumbled.

They parked their bikes and headed inside in search of Preacher. They found him at the bar with Dragon and Shadow.

"Who did it?" Preacher growled in greeting.

"We don't know," Steele told him. "Kid at the hardware store won't talk. I get the impression it's a woman."

"Lisa did it?" Preacher questioned.

"Don't know," Dagger shrugged. "She's fucking wacked. Thought I was there to get back with her. She evaded our questions, and I evaded her."

Steele chuckled. "Girls certainly out there. It could have been her, but I don't know."

"Fine," Preacher grumbled. "Hopefully this was a one-time thing."

Dagger turned to Steele once Preacher was done. "You mind if I borrow your truck tonight?" he questioned.

"Your bike acting up?" Steele inquired curiously.

"Nope," Dagger denied as he smirked. "I'm putting your genius idea into action."

Steele grinned back. "You know where to find her?"

"Nope, but I know her car. And with hair like that, she'll stand out," Dagger smirked.

"Good luck brother. I honestly think this could work," Steele told him as he threw him a set of keys. "Go find your girl."

Of course, that was when Lucifer and Dragon walked over to them.

"You got a date?" Lucifer asked.

"Not yet," Dagger denied. "But I hope to before the nights up."

"You can't date her for three more days," Lucifer announced. "That's the day I've got my money on."

"Nope," Shadow countered as he walked up. "See her tonight, but make the date for tomorrow."

Dragon had to add his two cents too. "I gave her a couple hours. You date her tonight, I'm winning this one for sure."

Dagger was ready to wrestle the bunch of them when Trike ran in.

"What's the matter?" Dagger asked, as the brother tried to catch his breath.

"Babies got colic. I've been staying with Misty to help. Am I too late to place a bet?" Trike huffed.

"Not much left," Steele warned.

"I'll take whatever you got," Trike grinned.

"Fucking bikers," Dagger growled as he stormed out the door. "My girl isn't going to shoot me."

He growled, when all he heard was the biker's laughter following him. Dagger stormed over to the truck and opened the door. Then he took off his vest and laid it on the back seat, where it would be out of sight. It was time to find his girl.

Chapter 11
Zoe

Zoe sat in the donut shop later that evening, drinking her apple juice and watching the strip club. It was almost five thirty, and she knew Mario would show up soon. The strip club opened at seven, but most nights he arrived around this time, and left an hour later. He wasn't there often when the club was open.

It still got dark early, so with the sun just setting, it was perfect. Zoe smiled when she saw him pull up and drive around the side. He always parked away from the street and close to the door. She grabbed her grocery bag and headed outside. She had been scoping the area, so she knew exactly where the cameras were.

As soon as she crossed the street, she pulled up the hood of her black hoody, and dropped her head so she faced the pavement. She zigzagged around the cameras and stayed in the shadows. Her eyes were everywhere as she glanced up and made sure no one saw her. With the strip club not opened yet, it was extremely quiet.

Zoe reached his car easily and grabbed a can of pink spray paint. She stood on her tiptoes underneath the camera so the lens wouldn't pick her up, popped the top, and sprayed each of the two cameras. Satisfied, she pulled out the industrial-sized box of Saran Wrap and got to work. Ten minutes later she was done and darting back across the street. This time she'd shopped two towns over for supplies. She wasn't taking chances.

Instead of going into the donut shop, Zoe darted around the back, and took off her hoodie. She picked up a backpack she had stashed there earlier, and shoved it in, along with the empty box. Then she slowly made her way back to her apartment and the storage unit. In no time at all, she had everything stashed away, and was inside changing.

Deciding to celebrate by going out to pick up dinner, she headed back outside. Zoe turned toward a burger place that wasn't too far away. She was almost there when a truck driving the opposite way suddenly veered across the road, and headed directly for her. She panicked when it stopped right in front of her. Then her mouth dropped open when the driver door opened, and Dagger stepped out.

"Hey Firecracker," he greeted with a grin. "I've been looking for you."

"You have?" she answered stupidly. Then she glared at him suspiciously. "Why?" she questioned.

"Because I want to take you out," he smirked.

"I don't date bikers," Zoe felt the need to remind him.

Dagger suddenly did a spin as he pointed to himself. "Look," he ordered. "No vest." Then he pointed to the truck. "No Harley. I'm not a biker tonight."

She blinked up at him, unsure. "What are you doing?" she asked warily.

"I'm asking you to get to know me as a regular guy. I'm asking you to forget I'm a biker, and forget what you think bikers are like, and to give me a chance." He stepped closer, and she leaned back to look up at him.

"I like you Firecracker, and you liked me too until you saw the vest. Please just give me a chance. If you still can't get past it after we've spent some time together, then as much as it will hurt me, I'll walk away."

Zoe stared at him in shock. The big badass biker was putting her feelings first. He was setting aside something important to him, just to have a chance with her. She was still frightened of bikers, and she knew his club was responsible for her sister's death, but he was hard to resist.

"One date," she nodded in agreement.

"Two dates, and we get to hold hands and smooch," Dagger grinned.

"Smooch?" Zoe questioned in surprise.

"Smooch, lock lips, suck face," he elaborated, then he stopped to study her. "What's your name?"

"Oh no," she denied. "I'm Firecracker to you. And if after two dates I decide to say no to you, I want a clean break. I can't do that if you know my name."

"What if I tell you my real name?" he pushed. She grinned, actually curious about that.

"You like to bargain," Zoe stated.

"Nope," Dagger told her. "I like to win."

"Oh lord," she grumbled as she followed him to the truck. He was definitely trouble.

Chapter 12
Dagger

Dagger couldn't believe that his Firecracker was sitting beside him. She had completely shocked him by agreeing. He was going to make the most of his two dates, and he was going to make her fall for him. He pulled into The Chicken Shack and turned to her.

"The Chicken Shack?" she asked in surprise. "It's our first date, and you're taking me to a place called The Chicken Shack."

"Hey," Dagger chuckled. "Don't knock it until you try it. Wait here, I'll be five minutes, and I promise you won't regret it."

Then Dagger moved quick, leaning over and kissing her cheek. He saw the surprise on her face, and before she could say anything, he jumped out and shut the door. He hurried inside, grabbed the takeout he had ordered, and hurried back out. He was both relieved and happy to see she was still in the truck.

"I half expected you to bolt," Dagger declared as he climbed back in and pulled out.

"The thought crossed my mind," she replied with a smirk.

Dagger chuckled, but said nothing more as he drove to the lake. Once there, he helped her out, grabbed the food, and caught hold of her hand. It only took a minute to reach the spot he had set up for them.

She stopped as soon as she saw it, and Dagger saw the surprise on her face. He had borrowed the white twinkly lights they used for the weddings, and strung them up in a tree. Then he had laid out a blanket. On the blanket was a bottle of wine chilling in a bucket, and a bouquet of flowers.

"Dagger," she sighed as she turned to him. "How?"

Dagger looked down at her and grinned. "I didn't know if you'd say yes, but I figured I'd get everything set up anyway. I like you Firecracker, and I'm going to make sure that after our two dates are up, you'll want to stay." Tears pooled in her eyes, and he immediately pulled her close.

"Dangerous," she whispered as she swiped at them with the back of her hand.

Dagger gave her a minute to compose herself, then he led her to the blanket, and they got comfortable. Leaning over, he grabbed a hoodie he had brought earlier, and wrapped it around her.

"It gets chilly here by the water once the sun goes down," he told her in explanation and she smiled at him.

"You know you aren't getting this back," she declared as she slipped her arms in.

He chuckled when her hands completely disappeared. Leaning over, he rolled up the sleeves, then handed her a plate. After dishing out some food, he handed her a mug he had filled with wine.

"Wineglasses will tip," Dagger told her when she looked at it curiously.

They ate, they laughed, and they kept the conversation light. Dagger didn't bring up the club once, and he made sure not to ask about her family. He didn't want anything on her mind except him. She was completely relaxed the entire time, and he loved that.

When it was getting late, and she started to yawn, he knew it was time to pack it up. It took him only a minute to take down the lights and put away the food. He took her hand again, after they'd divided up the supplies, and walked her back to the truck.

"Can I drive you home?" Dagger asked once they were seated inside.

"No," she whispered. "Drop me off at the donut shop."

"Firecracker, it's dark and that's across the street from a strip club. I wouldn't be much of a man if I left you there alone," he sighed.

"But how do I make a clean break if you know where I live?" she huffed.

"I don't think it would take me long to figure out where you live," Dagger admitted. "That hair of yours is memorable. All I have to do is ask around. It's a small town." She studied him a minute, then nodded, and he was grateful.

"I'm in the low apartment building a block from there," she admitted.

"That isn't a great area," Dagger frowned as he turned the truck in that direction. She didn't answer, and he sighed.

When he pulled up, he smiled at her. She slid across the seat and then got on her knees. She took him completely by surprise when she kissed him. The kiss was short, but Dagger loved it. Then he blinked when she grabbed her flowers and quickly got out, mimicking his earlier move at The Chicken Shack.

He laughed as he watched her run up to the apartment door. It was after she was inside when he realized she hadn't given him her number for their second date.

Chapter 13
Dagger

Dagger shot bolt upright from a sound sleep. Dazed, he turned and fell right off the bed. His back hit the floor and it knocked the breath out of him. What the fuck he thought, as he tried to figure out what was happening.

Suddenly a loud noise sounded from underneath his window. He covered his ears and crawled across the floor to retrieve his pants. Once he had them on, he looked at his alarm clock. It was five thirty in the morning. He grabbed his boots and shoved them on his bare feet, then hurried through the compound and outside.

When he stepped out, his mouth dropped open at the chaos he witnessed around him. Three roosters were running around the compound, and half-dressed brothers were chasing them. Of course, they were all yelling and crashing into each other. The girls stood back, and tears were running down their faces they were laughing so hard.

"Get them daddy," Catherine was yelling at Dragon as she clapped her little hands. She was two now, and she was the princess of the club.

It was obvious to Dagger the roosters were winning. The brothers were tiring and only getting more pissed off. One rooster stopped, threw back his head, and crowed. All the bikers dropped to their knees and covered their ears. The damn things were extremely loud this close up. Suddenly, Preacher and Navaho came storming out carrying blankets.

"Trike," Preacher yelled. "Get the fuck over here." The brother hurried to his side, and Preacher threw a blanket at him. "You're fucking fast. Get close to one and throw the blanket over its head," he ordered. Trike nodded, grabbed the blanket and took off.

"Give me one of those fucking blankets," Shadow yelled as he stormed towards Preacher. Raid immediately followed and took the third one off Navaho.

Five minutes later, the three roosters were caught. Navaho brought out a large box an engine had come in, and they dumped the roosters inside. Dagger was flabbergasted, this was the wildest shit he'd ever seen.

Then they turned, as Mario stormed down the path from his house, trailed by Trent, who was carrying his own box. A smiling Alex was following. Mario walked up to Preacher, opened the box, and threw an unconscious rooster on the ground.

"Look at its neck," Mario growled.

All the bikers crowded around, as Steele bent down and lifted its head. Around its neck was a bright pink collar.

"Please return to 145 Rose Meadow Lane," Steele read.

"Fuck, they're from local farms. Return the fucking things and find out who the hell took them," Preacher yelled.

"Why's yours asleep?" Catherine asked, as she peered over Dragon's shoulder.

"Because I punched it," Mario told her, and the little girl giggled.

"This goddamned shit needs to stop," Preacher growled. "First the gates, now roosters."

"And my car," Mario added.

Dagger looked his way. "What happened to your car?"

"Someone wrapped the entire thing in Saran Wrap. Do you have any idea how hard it is to get that shit off a car?" he complained. "I was peeling that crap off for two hours."

Dagger couldn't help it, he threw back his head and laughed. Of course, Mario just glared at him. When he calmed down, he turned to the brothers.

"Whoever's doing this obviously isn't out to hurt us," Dagger reminded them. "These are just pranks to piss us off."

"Well it's fucking working," Preacher snarled. "I was in bed with my Hummingbird, and I had to leave her to deal with this. That's not acceptable to me."

"Agreed," some of the brothers huffed.

"So, we get some sleep, then we meet for church and figure this out," Preacher ordered as he stomped away. "And somebody get rid of those roosters." All the brothers went to leave too, when Dragon turned back.

"You go on your date last night?" he questioned.

Dagger couldn't help but grin. "I certainly did."

"It went okay?" Dragon pushed.

"It was fucking perfect," Dagger told the brother.

"Good for you," Dragon replied. "I want my hundred bucks before the end of the day."

Dagger couldn't help it, he smirked at the brother. "I would have paid more. My Firecrackers worth it." Then he lost his smile when Lucifer spoke up.

"Five hundred says she's moved into his room by Thursday," Lucifer yelled.

Dagger walked away in annoyance as the asses placed more bets.

Chapter 14
Zoe

Zoe was completely confused. She had only known Dagger for an incredibly short time, but her feeling for him were strong, and they were only getting stronger. The date had been the best of her life. It was really easy to talk to him, and he was a lot of fun. He'd also gone out of his way to set everything up beforehand, which made him seem really invested in the date. She had been shocked that he had taken the vest off and was considerate of her feelings. She found it surprisingly easy to accept him as a regular guy and forget all about the fact he was a biker.

Zoe sat in the donut shop, drinking her apple juice and listening to the gossip. Her antics were spreading. She was now nicknamed the pink bandit, and she loved it. Customers were laughing about the roosters, and Mario's car was discussed through more laughter. Apparently, he hadn't been impressed. From the talk, she learned the roosters had been returned, and the farmers had kept quiet. Everyone liked the bikers, but they were having too much fun to let on who she was. The farmers hadn't even accepted her money, they just wanted her promise that they would return the birds unharmed.

Zoe finished her apple juice and headed out. She'd heard enough, and she was delighted. She walked down by the water and sat on a park bench. Someone sat down beside her, but she didn't pay them any mind. That is until her arm was grabbed forcefully. She turned, and when she did, she got a backhand to the cheek. Zoe cried out and looked to see a girl sitting beside her. The girl was stunning, but she looked furious. She leaned in close to Zoe, but Zoe couldn't move away with the grip she had on her arm.

"Talk around town is that you're interested in my Dagger. You've been seen with him several times, and I don't like that. I want to make it clear that he's mine. We've been together for a while, and he's going to make me his wife," she sneered.

Zoe just shook her head in confusion. Dagger didn't mention having a fiancé, and she wouldn't have gone out with him if she'd known.

"I've got someone watching you. If you go anywhere near him, I'll find out, and you'll pay. Nod in understanding," she ordered. Zoe immediately nodded.

Finally, the girl let go of her arm and stood. "You look like a smart girl. Keep this conversation quiet," she demanded before walking away.

Zoe sat there a minute, not understanding what had just happened. She had trusted Dagger, but it seemed he was like every other biker. She was glad she had only gone on one date with him, and she hadn't given out any information about herself. Her cheek throbbed, and she knew she'd have to go home and put ice on it.

Zoe stood and started toward her apartment. She was near tears and tried to hurry. She didn't need anyone to see her crying. She had really liked Dagger, and it hurt that he had been deceitful.

Zoe was almost home when she heard the sound of motorcycles. She picked up her pace, and started to jog, but the motorcycles pulled up right in front of her and blocked her path. There were three of them, but she only had eyes for Dagger. He climbed off and smiled at her, then his expression froze, as he got a look at her.

"What the fuck happened to you?" he growled, as he moved towards her. Immediately she backed up and held up her hand to stop him. Of course, that's when the tears fell.

"Don't you dare come any closer," she cried.

He immediately stopped, and his eyes turned wary.

"You lied to me," Zoe whispered. "I gave you a chance and you were lying to me."

"Firecracker, I have no idea what you're talking about. Tell me what you think I was lying to you about?" Dagger asked carefully.

"Your fiancé paid me a visit. Seems you forgot to mention her when we went out the other night. She wasn't happy about our date, and she was really clear about letting me know," she told him.

"I don't have a fiancé," Dagger growled.

"I don't care," Zoe cried. "You can forget about the second date." Then she darted around him and ran down the street. She heard his boots, but she only ran faster, because now the tears were streaming down near face.

Chapter 15
Dagger

Dagger was furious as he ran down the street after his Firecracker. The girl was fast, and he bet she'd give Trike a run for his money. What she said completely set him off, and the handprint on her cheek had seen him seeing red. He immediately knew she was talking about Lisa. That bitch had finally pushed him too far. He'd told her repeatedly that there would be nothing between them.

His girl had reached the apartment building, and she was shoving open the door. Dagger pushed himself hard, and just caught the door before it closed. She was already up one set of stairs, but she paused and looked back when she heard the door slam shut behind him. The tears on her face literally broke something inside him.

"Firecracker," Dagger begged. "Give me two minutes to explain and make sure you're okay."

She shook her head in the negative and turned away from him.

"I fucking care about you," he shouted in desperation. "I've finally found a girl that I can see myself spending the rest of my life with, and I'm not fucking letting a jealous nut job destroy it before it's even started."

Dagger sighed in relief when she stopped again. She didn't turn around, but he could tell she was listening.

"You're everything I want. You're smart, you're funny and you're fucking beautiful. You walk away from me now and I won't recover," he yelled.

"Why do you care so much? You don't even know me," she whispered through her tears.

"Our club believes there's one person who's put on this earth specifically for them. We know immediately when we find them. The first time I saw you, my heart fucking stopped. I need you, I can't fucking breath without you," Dagger admitted.

Her head dropped, and she looked defeated. "If I find out you're full of shit, I'm going to shoot you," she whispered. "Ive been through enough lately, and I'm barely holding on," she told him.

Dagger didn't waste a minute. He charged up the stairs, scooped her up, and kissed her head.

"You're ready to drop," he growled, when she looked at him in surprise. "Just lean on me for a bit."

He turned when the doors suddenly opened, and found Shadow and Wrench standing there. His Firecracker looked a little nervous, as she swiped at her tears and watched them.

"She okay?" Wrench questioned in concern.

"I'll make fucking sure she's okay. Do you think you can track down Lisa and hold her at the clubhouse? We need to set her fucking straight," he growled.

"We'll get her there," Shadow promised. Then the brothers slipped back out the door.

Dagger headed up the stairs and followed his girl's directions. After she leaned over and unlocked a door, he carried her inside. He stopped in astonishment when he got a look at the place. There were boxes lined up against one wall, and a mattress on the floor. His girl had some explaining to do. He carried her over to the mattress and sat her down. Then he went to her freezer, grabbed a small bag of corn, and wrapped it in a kitchen towel. He dropped to the mattress beside her and placed it gently on her cheek.

"I don't plan on staying long," she immediately blurted out. "I lost someone important to me, and I'm trying to figure out how to get past it."

"I can help with that," he told her. "But you need to tell me more."

"Not yet," she denied. "Tell me who Lisa is to you?"

Dagger signed, knowing he had to be honest with her. "She's a girl I dated for about a month. We didn't connect, and I knew it wasn't going anywhere. I broke it off and she didn't like that. She's got it in her head that she wants to be with a biker. I only just found out she was with another club member before me. I honestly think she's unstable," he told her.

"So, will you hurt her?" she questioned.

"Our club doesn't hurt women," he growled. "We'll figure this out without violence. We have a couple cops that can help us out," he admitted.

When her eyes went wide, he looked at her in confusion. "What?" he asked.

"You have cops that help you out," she said as she scooted back a bit. "So, they cover things up for you?"

Dagger stared at her in confusion. "What the hell have you been told about bikers?" he questioned.

Chapter 16
Zoe

Zoe stared at Dagger, not knowing what to say. He was asking about what she knew about bikers, and she wasn't ready to tell him the truth yet. If she gave him too much information, he'd end up figuring out who she was, and that it was her who was going after his club.

"I only know what I went through, and I'm not ready to tell you everything yet. Just know that bikers were involved in my family member's death," she told him.

"Firecracker, that's not telling me much. I'm trying to get to know you and figure this out, and you're not making it easy," Dagger sighed. "Are you saying that bikers killed your family member?"

"They did," she admitted sadly. She watched as he removed the corn, stood up, and thew it in the sink.

"Listen," he demanded as he leaned against the wall. "There are two different kinds of clubs. The bad ones are called one percenters. They run guns and drugs, they kill, they steal, and they give the rest of us a bad name. We are one of the other clubs. We make our money legitimately, we protect our family, and we protect our town. We have a couple detectives that are our friends. When somebody decides to go after our family, we take action. Sometimes people get hurt, but I promise you it's for a good reason. The detectives step aside sometimes," he explained.

"Give me an example?" she immediately demanded, wanting to understand better.

"One of our girls was kidnaped by a stalker. He tried to kill her by tying her up and setting the motel she was in on fire. We got her back, and the detectives helped," he told her. Her mouth dropped open in shock, but he wasn't done.

"Another of our girls was married before?" he imparted. "Her husband was extremely abusive. When she met Steele, she was in hard shape. Her husband stole all her money, raped her, and threw her down a well. We ended up blowing up a house, and the detectives helped cover it up."

"A well?" she cried.

"I think you need to meet the girls in our club. They're all sweethearts, and they've all gone through some terrible things. They could help you understand our club better. Maybe you should meet the detectives too. They could look into your relative's death for you," Dagger told her.

She studied him for a minute, then sighed. "I'm not sure about the detectives. If I do need help, I'd like to come to you first."

"Okay," Dagger agreed. "Now I need to go deal with Lisa, but I'd like to come back later tonight and check on you."

Then he sat beside her, pulled her into his arms, and kissed her. She was surprised, but she quickly leaned into him and kissed him back. The man certainly knew how to kiss. When he pulled back, she smiled up at him.

"We're doing more of that later. But we'll talk more too, and figure this out," he growled.

Then he was up and gone, and she was more confused than ever. What Dagger had said made sense, and she knew something wasn't right. If the club was a good one, why did they kill her sister. Maybe it was time to look into things more. She got up, changed and headed out.

Ten minutes later, Zoe was walking up to her sister's grave. She had tried to stay away, not wanting anyone to know who she was, but she really needed to be close to her. As she got close, she peered ahead, not believing what she was seeing.

When her sister died, she didn't have a lot of money. It had broken her heart, but she could only afford to put a small grave marker on her plot. Now, however, there was a beautiful headstone that looked extremely expensive in its spot. Her sisters name was on it in delicately carved script, and a beautiful rose was carved below it. Tears pooled in her eyes as she looked at it. Someone had spent a lot of money fixing her sisters grave up, and she needed to know who that was.

Zoe left the cemetery more confused than ever. She had inquired at the office, but they had just grinned and told her the person wanted to remain secret. Outside the gates she found two boys playing. She approached them with a grin.

"Do you boys want to get in on the stuff that's been happening to the bikers?" she asked. She grinned when both boys nodded excitedly. "Do you have any friends?" she questioned next.

Chapter 17
Dagger

Dagger parked his Harley near the clubhouse door and stomped into the common room. That witch Lisa had hurt his girl, and he wanted a piece of her. She'd also apparently been spreading the word around that she was his, and that wasn't ever happening.

"Where the fuck is she?" he yelled at the room in general. All the brothers stopped what they were doing and turned to look at him. "Tell me she's in the shed," he growled. He sighed when Preacher headed his way.

"Shadow called and told us about Lisa hitting your girl and claiming to be yours. I thought you set the bitch straight?" he pushed.

Dagger threw up his arms. "I thought I did too. The girls a nut job, there's no other way to explain it. When a pissed off biker tells you to back off, you fucking back off."

"I warned you she was a crazy one," Tripp grunted as he joined them.

"Well, you could have told me that before I hooked up with her. You know, maybe let a brother know about the weirdos in this town," Dagger huffed.

Tripp threw back his head and laughed. "So, what do I do about you?"

"Not fucking funny," Dagger roared.

"Look there are brothers out looking, but so far they've come up dry. Lisa probably knows she went too far and she's gone to ground," Preacher told him.

"Well, I want her in the fucking ground," he sneered.

"Sit down, the girls are at Misty's gushing over little Brady, so we're free to talk," Preacher demanded.

Chairs scraped as brothers dragged them over. It wasn't church, so whoever was there was included, and the rest could be filled in later. Dagger sat between Dragon and Lucifer, and the ass had the audacity to smile at him.

"It's actually kind of fun when it's someone else," Lucifer chuckled when Dagger raised his brow in question. Dagger raised his middle finger, flipping the brother off, then turned to Preacher.

"Any fucking leads on the kid that's pulling all these fucking pranks?" Preacher asked. "I'm fucking sick of this shit."

"The pink bandit," Lucifer helpfully supplied.

"The what?" Preacher demanded.

"The town calls the culprit the pink bandit," Lucifer clarified.

"Fucking hell," Preacher grumbled. "I'm not calling the kid that."

"It's kind of catchy," Sniper interrupted.

"Jesus, not you too," Preacher grunted. "Have we confirmed whether it's a fucking kid, someone with a grudge, or Lisa?"

"Lisa fucking makes the most sense," Tripp declared. "But honestly, these pranks take some thought, and I'm not sure she's fucking smart enough."

"I second that," Dagger added. "So, who's got a grudge?" he asked.

"We took out The Outlaws, and Trent looked into them pretty thoroughly after the shit with my Dewdrop and your sister. There's no one left," Dragon shrugged as he turned to Preacher.

"Parker's history, and Little Mouse's parents moved away," Steele added.

"We killed the prospect that hurt my sister, but there was another one," Sniper reminded them. "Adam, I think."

"No way," Dragon denied. "Adam was a decent guy who just made a mistake. Trent monitors him. He's working at a garage in another small town, and he keeps to himself. Got himself a pretty little girlfriend and everything."

"Chuck and Candy are dead, so it can't be them," Preacher told them. "What about someone with a grudge against Mario?"

"I can get him down here and ask," Steele pushed.

"Nah," Preacher objected. "Just give him a quick call and see if he can think of anyone."

"You're looking in the wrong direction," Wrench said, as he leaned forward and placed his arms on the table.

"Explain," Preacher demanded.

"I was a cop, I see things differently," Wrench imparted. "Your first assumption was probably right. It's a kid, most likely out to prove something. No one's been hurt and nothings been broken. If I held a grudge, I'd come in shooting. What I wouldn't fucking do is paint flowers on the gates."

"I completely agree," Tripp added. "What about your new girl Dagger?"

"What the fuck do you mean?" Dagger asked as he pushed his chair back.

"Relax," Tripp demanded. "It's just a question."

Wrench immediately backed up Tripp. "She's new to town. This shit started right after she arrived. She won't tell you her name, and she fucking hates bikers."

"One of her relatives was killed by a biker," Dagger growled, immediately defending his girl.

"Right," Tripp said. "So, she has a motive."

"It's not fucking her," Dagger snarled.

"Okay," Preacher shouted as he held up his hands. "I want men on the gates, day and night. I want everyone keeping their ears and eyes open. I want you out there asking questions. The fucking town knows something and I want to know what they know." Then Preacher turned to Dagger.

"Get some fucking information on your girl. If it's not her, you fucking prove it," he ordered.

Dagger pushed his chair back and headed to the door. "I'll fucking prove it," he snarled. "I find my one, and you fucking accuse her of this. You fuckers are a bunch of asses."

Then he slammed out the door and headed for his Harley. He was headed for his girl, and he was going to prove it wasn't her.

Chapter 18
Zoe

Zoe couldn't stop thinking about the things Dagger had said. If his club was so good, then who killed her sister. She was falling for Dagger, and it was killing her. Dagger was a part of that club, and if he had anything to do with her sister's death, then she would be heartbroken. She needed answers, and the first place she needed to start was with the detectives that had given her the information in the first place.

Zoe locked up her apartment, got into her car, and pulled out of the lot. She drove through town slowly and laughed when several of the kids she had dealt with earlier waved at her. They were all set up and ready to go, and she hoped that when she got back, the town would be talking again. She drove for an hour until finally stopping at a pay phone booth. She had driven two towns over to do this, as there weren't many pay phones left. She picked up the phone, inserted her coins, and dialled the police department. It only rang twice before it was answered.

"Haven police department, this is Colin, how can I help you?" a man on the other end answered. Zoe silently cursed for a minute. She knew it was Darren's partner, but she didn't know if he was crooked or not.

"Yes, I need to speak to either Candace or Charles," she told him.

There was silence for a minute, and then he answered. "I'm sorry honey, there's no one here by that name."

"But I was visited by two detectives from your department, and that was the names they gave me," Zoe argued.

"Well, I'm sorry to say that there's never been anyone working here going by either of those names. Are you sure you have the right department? There are several small towns in this area, and we all have our own departments," he told her.

She sighed. "You're Darren's partner, aren't you?" she asked.

"Yes, I am," he told her before he paused. "Can I get your name honey?" he suddenly asked.

"No," Zoe immediately told him. "I was visited by two detectives awhile back, and they gave me some disturbing information about a family member. I'm just trying to follow it up."

"Would you like to tell me what the information was?" he pushed. "Maybe I can help you."

"I don't want to reveal too much right now," Zoe admitted. "But I'm curious about Darren. How long have you been working with him? I understand he was Tripp's partner."

"I've been working with him for about three months now. He's a great guy. But what specifically are you asking?" he questioned curiously. She knew she was pushing her luck, but she had to get some answers.

"I've heard he works closely with The Stone Knight's," Zoe imparted. "I've also heard he covers things up for them, and that he may be crooked."

"That's a pretty big accusation," Colin replied carefully. "You sure you want to say that?"

Zoe dropped her head and leaned against the glass wall of the booth. "Listen," she pushed. "I'm trying to figure out the truth. I've recently lost someone close to me, and I heard the bikers were involved."

"Maybe you should meet with me, and we can talk in person," Colin advised.

"No," Zoe denied. "I'm talking to you now, and I'm really not comfortable even doing this."

"Okay," Colin finally conceded. "Listen, when I first started here, I actually thought Darren was covering things up for them. But I've learned a lot since then, and I've seen a lot. The club protects their women, and they love them with a kind of love I've never experienced. Sometimes these women are hurt and the law can't legally help them. The club does things their way, and Darren sometimes steps aside," he admitted. He paused a minute before continuing.

"At first I didn't agree with this. But I've seen first hand the things that happen to their loved ones, and I can't say I completely disagree. If I loved someone and someone hurt her, I'd do everything in my power to make that person pay," he admitted. "Wouldn't you?" Colin asked.

Zoe sighed, he completely had her. That was exactly what she was doing now.

"Darren's not a crooked cop," he assured her. "He just protects the people he cares about. The club does the same, and I can't find fault with that."

"Okay," Zoe said quietly. "I should hang up now."

"You need anything you come to me directly," he ordered. "It sounds to me like you may need help. I need to know though if you're in trouble?" he asked.

"I'm not in any trouble," Zoe assured him. "I'm just trying to figure some things out." Before he could say anymore, she hung up. She knew she had left him with a lot of questions, and she also knew he'd probably tell Darren about his conversation with her. It wouldn't take them long to figure out who she was. She'd made it clear to Dagger and a couple other bikers that she had a problem with them.

Signing, she left the booth and climbed back in her car. The conversation with Colin had only confused her more. Who the hell were Candace and Charles? Obviously, they weren't actual detectives. They hadn't looked like detectives, but she had been grieving over Amber at the time, and hadn't thought about it. Maybe she should figure that part out first. She was meeting many people in town, and they seemed to be really nice to her. Maybe she could ask them and see what they knew about things.

With a plan in mind, Zoe turned the car on, and headed back to town. One way or the other, she'd find out the truth about her sister's death.

Chapter 19
Dagger

Dagger searched all over for his Firecracker, but he had no luck. He was on his bike this time, and he was pissed. The brothers were accusing her of being the one to pull the pranks, and he didn't believe it. He knew both Tripp and Wrench had been cops, and they saw things that most people didn't, but this was his girl they were talking about. He'd had time to think about what they were saying, and it did look bad. She had arrived in town when the trouble started, and she did hate bikers, but it still didn't add up. There had to be more to it.

He pulled up to a light and stopped his bike. When he turned to the side, Tripp was pulling up beside him. Sighing, he nodded at the brother.

"I'm sorry," Tripp immediately apologized. "But everything fits with her."

"I know," Dagger told him sadly. "But I'll still defend her."

"Wouldn't expect anything less," Tripp agreed on a grin. "I'd do the exact same thing. But just remember the situation I was in. When my girl needed help, I didn't see it. We get tied up in our feelings. Maybe you're not seeing it either."

"Shit," Dagger cursed. "You have a point. If she is doing this, what the fuck do I do?"

"You find out why she's doing this," Tripp advised. "She lost a family member and bikers were involved. If it's her doing all this, she probably has a good reason. You have to hear her out first and not jump to conclusions like I did."

Dagger opened his mouth to respond, but the light changed. He sighed, lifted his feet, then took off.

Tripp followed behind him. They drove down the street and took the next corner. As soon as they passed a bush, about four kids jumped out aiming water guns at them. With nowhere to hide, they were soaked in seconds. Both swore as they kept going, and the kid's laughter followed them. When they got a safe distance away, they pulled over.

"Goddamn," Tripp complained. "I'm fucking soaked through."

Dagger peeled his shirt from his body and twisted the front to ring it out. "Were those fucking super soakers?" he growled.

Just then, two more kids ran out from behind a building, and they each threw a water balloon. Their aim was perfect, and again Dagger and Tripp were hit.

"Fucking hell," Dagger growled.

Pissed, he pulled out and roared in the direction of the clubhouse. He wasn't sitting around making it easy on the fuckers. When they pulled up to the gates and drove inside, they found a lot of bikers standing in the courtyard. They were all as wet as them, and none of them looked happy.

"We're giving up the search for now," Lucifer was telling Preacher. "Those fuckers are everywhere."

Dagger and Tripp immediately headed over.

"I think every kid in town has water guns and water balloons," Lucifer complained.

Navaho headed his way, and the brother looked worse than all of them. His hair was dripping, and he actually sounded like he was squishing when he walked. He stopped beside them, kicked off his boots, and literally dumped the water out of them.

"I got off my bike," he informed them with a frown. "Kid was hanging out a window. Dumped an entire bucket over my head."

Dagger couldn't help it, he threw his head back and laughed. He'd thought he got it bad, but Navaho looked ridiculous.

"I still haven't forgotten the leaf blower incident. I'd stop fucking laughing if I were you," Navaho growled at him.

Dagger immediately sobered. The fucker had chased him for fifteen minutes that day.

"So, we're hiding in the compound now?" Tripp questioned. "Because it's going to be hard to get answers that way."

"Maybe we should get water guns of our own and retaliate," Dagger chuckled.

"This isn't fucking funny," Preacher yelled. "Go out in trucks and vans, but get this done."

"I'm changing first," Dagger complained. "But I still haven't found my girl. And we still haven't found Lisa."

"Well you've got a place to start," Preacher declared.

Then they all stared as Ali, Tiffany and November walked up. "What are you three doing?" Preacher said in exasperation.

"You need answers, and obviously people won't talk to you. You're probably going up to them growling and showing your muscles," Tiffany sighed.

"Right," November agreed. "You need sweet girls to get them talking."

Dagger couldn't help it, he started laughing again. "You ran out in a gun fight yelling at a psychopath. How the fuck are you sweet?"

"Hey," she said, turning angry eyes towards him. "I bet we get answers before you do."

"One hundred dollars," Tiffany yelled, as she stole Preachers wallet and pulled out a bill.

"Fucking women," Dagger grunted as he turned and walked away.

Chapter 20
Zoe

Zoe took her time heading back home. She stopped in the town just before hers and headed into the local diner. It was getting late and she was getting hungry. After hanging up with Colin, she had decided to do a little shopping before she headed back. Just because she was starting to question the things the two detectives had told her, didn't mean she was letting up at all. No matter what, Amber had been killed in Haven, and she had worked for Mario and the bikers. That meant that even if she found out they were innocent, they still knew about her death.

Zoe walked into the diner and took a seat in a small booth by the window. Immediately a waitress came up and placed a menu on the table in front of her. "My name's Karen", she greeted. "I'll be back in just a sec with a glass of water, and I'll take your order then."

Zoe smiled at the girl. "Sounds great," she told her.

Karen smiled back and was off again, so Zoe scanned the other people in the diner. Most were sitting at tables and chatting. It surprised her to see how busy it was. Then she noticed a couple people at a table not too far away laughing and showing each other their phones. As she looked around, more customers seemed to be concentrating on their phones. When Karen made her way back to the table, she was chuckling.

"What's so funny?" Zoe asked curiously.

"Oh, there's someone in Haven pranking The Stone Knight's," she explained. "Those big softies are driving themselves foolish trying to figure out who's doing it."

"Big softies?" Zoe questioned.

"Yep, those bikers are the most decent fellas around. They do a lot for the community, and they help out where they can. And when they fall in love, it gets even worse. They follow their girls around like puppy dogs. I only wish I could catch one for myself," she sighed. "I'd like to have one of those sweethearts treat me like I was the only thing that mattered."

Zoe huffed, realizing another person was telling her something that contradicted what she'd heard.

"So, they don't know who's pranking them?" she questioned.

"They don't have a clue," Karen chuckled. "The latest thing the pink bandit did was arm all the kids in Haven with water guns and send them out in the streets. The pictures I've been shown me in the last few minutes would make anyone laugh."

Zoe smiled in satisfaction. After talking for another minute, she placed her order, and Karen left. She was thrilled her plans were going so well, and it seemed like everyone was having fun with it. She had really been afraid that the town would side with the bikers, and that would have made everything harder. When her meal came, she ate quietly, and watched the people around her. It was hard not to laugh with them.

When she was done, she gave Karen a decent tip, and and headed out to her car. Zoe knew the bikers would be looking for her even harder now, and that worried her. She also knew Dagger had said he'd visit her later, and she wasn't sure what to do about that. She was falling for the guy, but she was concerned about what he'd do if he found out that she was pink bandit. Zoe knew he cared about her, he'd made that crystal clear, but she also knew he cared about the club. She didn't want to see what he'd do if he had to take sides, because he'd been with the club a long time, and he'd only talked to her a handful of times.

When Zoe finally pulled back into town, a couple boys came running up to her car. She stopped at the side of the road to greet them. She couldn't stop laughing with them, as they told her about getting some of the bikers. She loved that the boys were having so much fun. Climbing out of her car she headed for the trunk.

"You boys feel like doing something else?" Zoe asked.

She laughed at the enthusiasm they responded with. When she opened the trunk, the boys starting laughing. It didn't take her long to say her goodbyes and send them on their way, all loaded down with supplies. She watched as other boys ran up to them and helped them with their burdens. This would be so much fun she thought, as she jumped in her car and headed to her apartment.

Chapter 21
Zoe

Instead of heading home, Zoe went to the lake. She didn't go to the normal spot the locals went to, instead she headed down a long dirt road, and stopped at a fairly secluded spot. One of the farmers she had borrowed a rooster from told her about this. She didn't want to run into the bikers, and she wanted more time to herself. She pulled into the tiny parking lot and sighed in contentment when there were no other cars there. Getting out, the sun immediately warmed her skin, and the breeze ruffled her long hair. She followed the path to the water and was surprised by how pretty it was.

Zoe looked across the lake and knew the bikers had their compound there, but with the lake being so big, she couldn't see it. The beach on this side was fairly long, and the water was calm. She took off her shoes, threw them up the shore a bit, and waded into the water. The bottom of her pants got a bit wet, but she didn't care. The cool water on her bare feet was worth it. She hoped her sister had known about this spot, because she knew it was one she would have enjoyed. Thinking of her sister always made her sad, the ache in her heart wasn't easing at all. People told her it would get better with time, but she didn't believe them.

Zoe wandered the shore for hours, getting lost in the water, pretty beach rocks, and sand. Finally, she sat down, watching as the sun started to set. She knew she'd have to head home, but she was reluctant to leave. Her thoughts slowly returned to the club. The guys were smart, and she knew it wouldn't be much longer until they figured out it was her pulling all the pranks. It might be time to call it quits and move on. The only other option was to pull more serious ones, and she wasn't sure if she wanted to do that.

Zoe still had questions about their involvement, but even if she didn't, she wasn't out to hurt anybody. If she upped the anti, she knew that was exactly what could happen. Then there was the Dagger issue. She wasn't any closer to finding a solution to that either. She was falling for him, and she thought about him more and more all the time. He was definitely someone she could spend her life with.

Sighing, Zoe climbed to her feet, and went back to her car. In minutes, she was headed back down the road towards her apartment. Of course, she took the route that would take her past the compound. No one knew her car except Dagger, so she figured she was safe. As soon as she got close, she started laughing. Cars were parked at the side of the road and people were taking pictures. Every tree was covered in pink toilet paper, and it looked awesome. Even the gate had it thrown over the top. The bikers were out there cursing up a blue storm and trying to pull it all down. She knew it would take them at least another couple hours to get it all. The boys had done a fantastic job.

Zoe drove straight past and didn't stop, and thankfully nobody noticed her. Another ten minutes and she was pulling into the parking lot of her apartment. She was still smiling as she got out of her car and started towards the door. She was almost there when strong arms lifted her off the ground. One arm went around her waist, and another went around her neck. She tried to struggle and scream, but the arm around her neck tightened, and she found it hard to breathe.

Zoe cried as he carried her into the trees at the back of the lot. She actually breathed a sigh of relief when she was thrown to the ground. She gulped in air quickly and looked around. No one was around, and she was too far from the building to be seen or heard. She pushed to her feet and started to run, when she was hit in the back of her head. She fell, and stars danced between her eyes.

"I have a message from Lisa," a man breathed into her ear. Then a white-hot fire seared her lower back. She screamed in pain as the man spoke again. "Dagger is hers."

Then he was gone, and Zoe was left alone, bleeding in the woods. She tried to stand, but the pain only intensified. The black spots got bigger and there was nothing she could do when finally, she passed out.

Chapter 22
Dagger

Dagger was furious. He had driven all over town, and still there was no sign of his Firecracker, or of Lisa. He needed to find Lisa, but his Firecracker was his priority. With the slap she had taken from his ex, he had no clue how she felt now. He hoped she still wanted to see him, but he was afraid she had run from him. A crazy ex was something he knew most girls wouldn't put up with.

Dagger circled the town twice, and there was no sign of her. He even stopped people on the street, but no one had seen her. He had gone to her apartment twice already, but he headed there again.

Maybe he had just missed her. When he pulled into the back lot, he was happy to see her little car there. Dagger parked right beside it and immediately headed towards the apartment building. He rang the buzzer and waited, but she never answered. He knew then she was probably avoiding him.

Sighing, Dagger gave up and left. His nut job ex had most likely succeeded in driving her away. He had to consider that his Firecracker may never want to see him again. He'd give her one more day, and then he was waging war. That girl was his, and he knew she had liked him. He had explained the Lisa situation and she had listened. He wasn't accepting the cold shoulder from her now.

Dagger stormed down the stairs and headed back to the compound. He needed to know if Lisa had been found yet. He pulled up to the gates and was happy to see all the toilet paper was gone. There were no cars parked out front, and no one was taking fucking pictures. He pulled through the gates and stopped close to the clubhouse. When he went inside, he saw that most of the bikers were there.

"Any word on Lisa or your girl?" Preacher immediately questioned. Dagger sat beside his prez at the bar and grabbed the shot glass Smoke placed in front of him. He threw it back and then dropped his head.

"I can't find either of them, and it's pissing me off. I think you're right about Lisa hiding, but I think now my Firecracker may be hiding too," he complained.

"She give you any indication she was done with you?" Steele asked as he joined them.

"No," Dagger replied. "I honestly thought I got through to her. She listened to me, and she seemed happy when I mentioned I'd stop by again tonight."

"So, you know where she is?" Preacher inquired.

"Yeah," Dagger grumbled. "It looks like she's at her apartment, but she won't open the door."

"Maybe you should give her some time," Steele declared. Dagger glared at him.

"That what you did with Cassie?" Dagger questioned angrily.

"Hell no," Steele smirked. "I pushed until I was all she could see."

"Exactly," Dagger replied. "So, I can't give her time to get into her head."

"So, head the fuck back there and get the landlord to let you in," Preacher told him.

Dagger stood, he didn't even say a word, he just headed back out the door and got on his bike. Ten minutes later he was back at her apartment and banging on the landlord's door. It took the fucker five minutes to answer. When he finally did, Dagger glared at him.

"I need to get into my girlfriend's apartment," he explained. "The redhead on the fourth floor."

The ass smirked. "She kick you to the curb?" he questioned.

Dagger turned furious eyes on the man. "I wouldn't fuck with me right now. I've had a long day, and I haven't been in a good fight in a while."

The man immediately paled. He pulled a key chain from his pocket, headed up the stairs, and silently unlocked her door. Dagger moved into the apartment and looked around. It was getting darker, and not a single light was on. He moved around anyway and checked both the bathroom and bedroom. They were empty. His girl wasn't there.

"She could be at the shed," the landlord suggested. Dagger turned to him in question.

"The shed?" he repeated.

"Yep. She pays me to store stuff in the run down shed out back. She could be in there," he explained.

"Show me," Dagger growled.

He followed the man back down the stairs, out the door, and around the building. Sitting at the side of the parking lot was indeed a shed. As they approached, Dagger saw a padlock on the door. His girl wasn't here either, it was locked tight.

"You got a key for this one?" Dagger asked.

"Nope," the man denied. "She's a cute little thing, and she explained she had lost a relative. Told me she wanted to store some of her sister's stuff in here."

Dagger stopped dead. "Her sister?" he growled.

"Yeah, said she died a while ago. Didn't explain how though. When she asked for all the keys, I gave them to her," he shrugged. "Girl looked broken."

"Thanks," Dagger acknowledged as he headed back to his bike. Finally, he had a piece of the missing puzzle, and he knew that one bit of information could be just what he needed.

Chapter 23
Dagger

Dagger pulled up to the clubhouse once more. When he walked in the door, he headed back to the bar and to Preacher. He was happy to see more brothers there, as he needed everyone's help on this one. As soon as he got close, Preacher raised a brow in question.

"I need help," Dagger requested. "Can we get Mario and Trent down here?" Preached turned to Steele and nodded, and Steele moved away to make the call.

"You have something?" Preacher questioned, giving him his full attention.

"I think so," Dagger sighed. "It's something the landlord told me. I want to pool all my resources and get everybody on this."

"Okay, let's move to a table and talk. If we have enough information, we can move to church," Preacher declared as he stood and took his beer to a nearby table. Steele ended his call and joined them, and so did Dragon, Shadow and Sniper.

"I want Tripp and Wrench in on this too," Dagger added. "Their backgrounds may help."

Steele nodded and again picked up his phone. Another whiskey was placed in front of him, and he nodded at Smoke as he walked away. He downed it, then waited for everyone to arrive. A few minutes later Trent, Mario, Tripp and Wrench had joined them.

"Tell us what you have," Preacher ordered.

"I went by my girl's apartment. Her car was there, but she wasn't. I found the landlord and was told that she had rented a storage shed behind the building," Dagger explained.

"You found something in it?" Dragon questioned.

"No," Dagger told them. "It was padlocked, and the landlord didn't have a key. But he told me that my girl had recently lost a sister, and she was using the shed to store some of her sister's stuff."

"A sister," Steele grunted in surprise. "So, this would be the dead relative that she thinks the bikers killed?"

"Thinks?" Dagger asked in confusion.

"She hasn't told you anything, and nothings been confirmed. I'm not taking her word for it without proof," Steele grumbled.

Dagger immediately pushed his chair back and slammed his fists on the table. "That's my fucking girl you're talking about."

Preacher moved between them and raised his hand. "Then let's get the proof," he conceded.

"So, if it's her sister who died," Tripp cut in, "then she has a motive. I still think it's her pulling the stunts. Kids can't afford to pay for the amount of paint that was needed to paint the gates. Farmers would never give up their roosters to kids. And I don't think kids could cover a car in Saran Wrap and not draw any attention."

"I agree," Wrench added. "You know of any girls that were killed by the club. She could be Carly's sister or maybe Candy's."

"Carly didn't have any sisters," Sniper growled. "And she's in jail, not dead."

"Right, so what about Candy? We didn't know Chuck was her stepdad, she could have half sisters we don't know about," Tripp imparted.

Just then Preacher's cell rang. He answered it, grunted 'send them in', and hung up. "Darren and Colin are headed in," he explained.

Dagger turned to the door and watched as the detectives headed inside. Colin's eyes lit on Dagger, and he headed their way. After they were seated, Colin explained why they were there.

"Got a phone call this afternoon," he told them. "A girl was asking about the club. Wanted to know if you guys were legit or one percenters. Also asked if Darren was on the take."

"Jesus," Dragon cursed. "You get a name?"

"No, but she said bikers killed a relative, and she was trying to figure shit out," Colin said. "Sound familiar?"

"Fuck," Dagger roared. "It was my Firecracker."

"Sounds like it," Colin agreed.

"So, who the fuck was her sister?" Dagger questioned.

Colin was about to answer, when the doors were thrown open so hard, they bounced off the wall. All the brothers turned to see Snake standing there. The brother had been manning the gate.

"You're going to want to see this," he explained as he headed back out and across the lot.

Chairs pushed back, and boots hit the floor as every biker there followed Snake. In minutes they were standing at the opened gates and staring into the faces of about fifty very angry boys.

Chapter 24
Dagger

Dagger stared at the boys in confusion. They looked like they were all ready to do battle, and Dagger was actually a bit worried. He looked at his brothers, but it looked like they had no idea what to do either. When a truck pulled through the gates, the boys were forced to move aside, and Dagger was actually relieved. Ali, Tiffany and November stepped out, and they looked grim.

"Did you have any luck?" Dagger immediately questioned, turning his attention away from the boys.

"We didn't find either one of them. But an old lady saw your girl get out of her car at the apartment. She looked down for a minute, and when she looked back up, your girl was gone. She said it was only a quick minute, there was no way she could have crossed the parking lot in that amount of time. She said your girl just up and disappeared," Ali told him.

Dagger was instantly uneasy. That didn't sound very good.

"Hey bikers," the tallest of the kids yelled, gaining all their attention.

"The streetlights are on," Dagger yelled. "Shouldn't you all be in bed or something?"

"You got our girl," the kid immediately yelled back, scowling at him. "And we aren't leaving without her."

"What the fuck are you talking about?" Preacher growled in annoyance. "We don't have time for this."

"Well make time," the little shit yelled back.

Preacher was about to yell again, when Macy appeared and placed her hand on his arm. He looked down at her, and it seemed like all the tension left him.

"Hummingbird," he sighed. She smiled up at him and then turned towards the boy.

"Who's missing honey?" she softly asked. The boy looked at her and instantly deflated.

"You promise not to get mad?" he asked, and Macy nodded her head. "We help the girl called the pink bandit pull off her pranks."

"A bunch of kids and a girl are besting the big badass bikers?" November snickered. "This is great."

"I don't think now's the time to point that out," Lucifer cautioned as he moved protectively in front of her. Wrench appeared from thin air suddenly and moved to her side. She looked between her man and her brother and didn't say anymore.

"Why are you here?" Macy questioned. All the boys held up water guns, and the brothers all took a step back. None of them were interested in getting wet again.

"She's missing," the boy sneered. "And we figure you found out it was her and took her. We came to get her back."

Macy looked back at Preacher, and the prez slowly prowled to her side. One boy suddenly shot him in the chest. Preacher looked down at the wet spot and growled.

"Sorry?" the boy warily apologized. "You moved and I got nervous."

"Who the fuck is the girl?" Preacher questioned through gritted teeth.

The boys all looked at each other, and Preacher signed. "We don't have her here, and we still have no idea who's doing it."

"She has red hair," the boy finally admitted. "She was supposed to meet us tonight, but she never showed."

Dagger stood there shocked for a minute, then turned and ran for his bike. He didn't care what his Firecracker was doing, all he heard was that she never showed. He got a bad feeling in his gut, and he wasn't ignoring it.

"Where the fuck are you going?" Preacher yelled.

Dagger stopped for a minute to answer. "I'm going to find my girl. I got a bad feeling and that fucking terrifies me. I'll start at her car and search the parking lot. If the old lady said she disappeared quickly, then that's our best bet."

"Smoke, Wrench, get a couple vans. Load up these kids and take them back to town. Steele, you and Cassie follow in the truck, call Doc at the hospital and put him on standby. Shadow grab a medical bag in case we need it. Let's mount up," Preacher yelled.

Dagger nodded his head in thanks, then turned away. In minutes he was on his Harley and headed out, with most of the brothers behind him. He pushed his bike and completely ignored the speed limit. In ten minutes, he was pulling in beside his

Firecracker's car. He looked at the car closely and noticed it was unlocked. Most girls would lock their cars as soon as they got out of it. He looked at the pavement and started to search. It only took him a minute to find a set of keys that had to belong to his girl. He held them up for the brothers to see.

Preacher scanned the parking lot. "We start with the woods at the back of the lot. If anyone gets a trail, yell for Navaho."

Dagger didn't waste anytime. He sprinted across the lot and was the first one in the woods. He'd find his girl, and he wouldn't stop until she was safe.

Chapter 25
Zoe

Zoe woke slowly, surprised that it had gotten so
dark. She was really heartbroken to see she was still
in the woods behind her building. She kind of had
hope that she'd wake up in a hospital, of course she
wasn't that lucky. There was also the little fact that
no one knew she was missing. Dagger had said he'd
come back, but when he couldn't find her, he
probably just left again. She was supposed to meet
the boys, but they probably just figured she was
busy and would find them later.

Zoe had tried earlier to stand and head for the
parking lot, but the pain had been too much and

she had passed out. She knew it had been a knife the man had plunged into her back, but she had no idea how deep it had gone. She was cold, but then the sun was down, and she was covered in wet, sticky blood. She could move her legs, and she had stood for a minute, so she knew it was safe to say the damage hopefully wasn't too bad.

Zoe had known Lisa was crazy right away, but she never in a million years would have thought the ex would go this far. How Dagger could have ever dated her, blew Zoe's mind. The girl had been stunning, but he had to have seen her crazy underneath. She had no idea what to do, as she had a feeling that this was just another warning. If she ever saw Dagger again, she'd have to tell him.

Zoe decided right then and there that she was done with the pranks. She was tired and frustrated, and figured maybe it was time to just come right out and ask Dagger if he knew anything about her sister's death. She had to trust that he'd be completely honest with her. And she had to trust that the same thing didn't happen to her.

Zoe worried about what his reaction to her confession would mean. Would he have to choose between the club and her? She hoped not, because they'd only known each other for a couple days. She couldn't see him picking her. And, if she was honest with herself, she didn't want him to have to make that choice. If it came down to it, she'd leave.

Zoe was face down in the dirt, and couldn't see much, but she could hear. She knew a motorcycle when she heard it, and she heard a ton of them headed her way, or at least she hoped they were headed her way. Then the ground started to shake, and she trembled right along with it. She knew without a doubt that from how close the sound was, they were pulling into her buildings parking lot. She almost cried when the rumble finally stopped and shouting ensued.

It sounded like all the bikers were shouting 'Firecracker' at the same time, and she knew they were there for her. Tears rolled down her cheeks as the voices got closer, but she was too weak to do more than whisper Dagger's name. Feet pounded in every direction, and then they all stopped. She held her breath as someone shouted 'Navaho'. Then it seemed like they all started to move together, and they were all headed her way.

"Dagger," Zoe cried out as she dragged her body towards the nearest tree. When she was close, she grabbed onto it, and tried to pull herself up. Searing pain shot through her back and she cried out. She turned her head, and found herself staring at a very large, very good looking native Indian. Zoe barely had time to register him, when he was knocked out of the way and Dagger was suddenly there. But so were over a dozen other bikers, and they quickly surrounded her. She concentrated on the biker she was falling for, as he dropped to his knees beside her. He reached out for her, and she held up a hand to stop him.

"Firecracker?" he questioned in concern. "I really need to hold you right now."

"Zoe," she whispered brokenly. "My name's Zoe."

Dagger blinked a couple times, then grinned at her. "Prettiest name I've ever heard."

"Is there a doctor with you?" she whispered. "I've been stabbed in the back and I think I'm going to pass out again now," she advised him.

Zoe watched as his face drained of colour, and heard him as he roared her name, but the black spots were getting bigger and there was no fight left in her. She gave in, and slumped back down, knowing Dagger would take care of her.

Chapter 26
Dagger

Dagger stared at his girl as her eyes closed and she passed out. His heart literally froze as he realized what she had said.

"Did she just say she was stabbed in the fucking back?" Dagger roared. "Shadow," he yelled as his head rose and he scanned the surrounding brothers. He grabbed his Firecrackers hand, not sure where else it was safe to touch her.

"I'm here," Shadow assured him, as he pushed his way in and dropped to his knees beside him. Immediately he opened a bag and started routing through it. "Flashlights," he yelled, "I need flashlights on the girl and my bag." Most of the brothers had brought one to help with the search, so they aimed them where Shadow asked.

"Was she mobile when you found her?" Shadow asked, as he carefully lifted her shirt. Dagger panicked when the lights revealed how much blood soaked her shirt.

"It looked like she was trying to pull herself up using the tree," Navaho supplied.

"Good," Shadow replied. "That means her spine wasn't affected at all. I'll cover the wound, but she needs Doc. I don't know what kind of internal damage was done, and she's lost a shit ton of blood."

Dagger shuffled even closer and leaned down to place his mouth near her ear. "You'll be okay, Firecracker. I promise to take care of you from now on. You're mine now," he vowed.

Zoe opened her eyes a slit and looked at him. "Yours," she whispered. "I'm yours." Then her eyes closed again.

"Jesus Shadow, hurry up," Dagger pleaded. Shadow nodded and got back to work. When he was done, he turned to him again.

"Pick her up, just be careful, she's still bleeding," Shadow cautioned.

Dagger picked her up as gently as he could and cradled her against his chest. "She's so cold," he told them worriedly.

Shadow placed his hand on his shoulder. "She'll be okay brother. She's lost a lot of blood, and she's wet, but I promise you she'll be okay."

Dagger eyed him a minute, then nodded. He turned back towards the parking lot and moved at a fast clip out of the woods. As soon as they cleared the trees, all the brothers stopped at the sight before them. Once more the boys stood there eyeing them.

"We needed to know she was okay," the same boy that had spoken before told them.

Dagger immediately thought this kid was the shit. "What's your name?" he asked.

"Jacob," the boy said a little hesitantly.

"How old are you Jacob?" Dagger questioned.

"I'm fourteen," he responded.

"You turn eighteen and you think the biker lifestyle appeals to you, you come see me," Dagger ordered. "You probably saved my girls life tonight Lion."

"Lion?" the boy asked.

Dagger was moving again towards Steele's truck as he answered. "You're brave like a lion. Took on a whole biker club to protect someone you care about. You also roared at us like a lion. It fits," he explained.

The boy stared at him a minute, then grinned. "You'll see me again," Lion yelled.

Dagger climbed in the backseat, and Steele took off like a shot. It took five minutes to get to the hospital, and Steele pulled right up to the door.

Doc was there to greet him, and Dagger was thankful. He climbed out the vehicle, still holding his Firecracker, and hurried after Doc.

"Shadow called me and gave me a run down of her condition. I've got an operating room waiting. I need to know if they hit anything vital," Doc grunted.

Then before he knew it, she was pried from his arms and placed on a gurney. He could only watch as they rushed her into a room, and he was being pushed away. A hand grabbed his arm, and he looked back to see Dragon pulling him away.

"Let Doc work," Dragon ordered. "Your Firecracker will be just fine."

Dragon led him down the hall to the waiting room and made him sit. In minutes, the room was full. Dagger simply dropped his head and stared at the floor.

"You know who did this?" Preacher asked, as he took the seat beside him.

"No," Dagger huffed. "But Lisa slapped her earlier and warned her to stay away from me. It could be her, or it could be a fucker who likes to hurt girls."

Preacher nodded. "We'll have to wait until she wakes then."

"Her name's Zoe," he told Preacher. "She told me tonight before she passed out."

"Zoe," Mario growled from the other side of the room. Then he was pushing off the wall and headed their way. "Amber's sister was named Zoe."

Dagger's head snapped up and he stared at Mario in surprise. "Jesus Christ," he cursed, as everything started to make sense.

Chapter 27
Zoe

Zoe woke slowly, to realize she was lying on her stomach and she was really warm. She moved carefully and winced as pain shot up her spine.

"Easy Firecracker," Dagger growled from below her. "You move too much and you'll pull your stitches."

She blinked and looked down into Dagger's worried face. Lifting her head, she immediately realized she was in the hospital. She groaned and dropped back onto his chest.

"Isn't there some sort of rule that you're not supposed to be in a hospital bed with me," Zoe asked.

"Do I look like someone who follows rules?" Dagger chuckled. "And besides, I had to hold you."

"I think I needed to be held as much as you needed to hold me," she admitted. "How bad am I hurt?" she questioned as she burrowed in closer to him.

"Doc said the knife hit some muscle and just missed your spine. He sewed up the damaged tissue and stitched it closed. He also gave you a blood transfusion. There shouldn't be any permanent damage, but you will have to take it easy for a while," Dagger told her. She sighed, knowing she could have died out there.

"Doc also advised you move into the clubhouse with me," Dagger continued. "He said you should sleep on my chest every night so you don't accidentally hurt your back."

Zoe smirked into his neck. "He did, did he?" Then something else occurred to her. "How in the world did you find me?"

"You can thank your minions for that," Dagger replied with a frown. She looked up at him in confusion.

"About fifty boys showed up at the clubhouse and threatened us with water guns," he explained.

"Oh my god," Zoe cried. "I was supposed to meet them." Then she covered her mouth, realizing what she had said.

Immediately Dagger pulled her hand away and brought it to his mouth to lay a tender kiss on her palm. She melted, even though she was terrified about what she had revealed.

"I know you have a reason for what you did, and honestly I don't fucking care. You're my girl now, and I'm fucking behind you. You didn't hurt anyone, and I'm fucking proud of your ingenuity. You belong with me," Dagger growled.

A tear ran down her cheek and he reached up to brush it away. "You really don't care that I went after your club?" Zoe asked in surprise.

"What part of me saying you have to move in with me confused you?" he asked with a raised brow.

She giggled, then shimmied up him, and placed her lips against his. And just like before, he immediately took over. When he pulled back, she was breathless.

"I really hate to interrupt," Doc called from the doorway. "But I wondered if you'd like to head home. I'm assuming you're taking her to the clubhouse so I can keep an eye on her there?" he asked.

"Ummm," Zoe said hesitantly. "I don't know if I'm welcome there."

"I carry dynamite everywhere I go," Dagger told her. "The brothers know not to mess with me."

"Okay," she agreed quietly. "I'm really curious about that statement, but I'm not sure if I want to know."

"All in due time," Dagger smirked as he gently rolled out from under her and climbed off the bed.

"Where's your shirt?" Zoe asked in surprise.

"You're wearing it," he told her. She looked down, and sure enough she was now covered in the black shirt he had been wearing earlier.

"I don't have any pants on," Zoe whispered hesitantly.

"Here," Doc called as he threw a pair of scrub pants Dagger's way. "Drawstring waist."

Dagger smirked at her once Doc had left. "Come on Firecracker," he ordered. "This will be fun. I've never actually helped a girl get into her pants before."

Zoe immediately covered her ears. "I don't need to know that."

It took longer than she thought to get into the pants, and she was sweating by the time Dagger was done. He carefully picked her up and cradled her against his chest. When he walked into the hall, it surprised her to see it was full of bikers. Nervously, she looked up at Dagger. Just then, the biker she knew was Preacher stepped forward.

"It's nice to meet you Zoe. We'll escort you back to the clubhouse, and then we need to talk," Preacher greeted.

"Okay," she whispered, then was shocked when he winked at her and turned away.

Chapter 28
Dagger

The ride back to the clubhouse was quiet. His Firecracker stared out the window at all the bikes. She seemed both amazed by the sight of them and horrified at the thought of what was to come. He knew she was expecting the worst, and it bothered him. His club would never hurt her for a couple pranks. Preacher had also winked at her, which was a good sign that he wasn't angry at her. Dagger knew he had been, but once he found out who she was, it had deflated.

He still couldn't believe that she was Amber's sister. It was someone the club hadn't even thought about, and they all had known about her. They had been looking for sisters of the people that had wronged them, and they had killed. Amber hadn't even been on their radar.

As they pulled up, Dagger parked, and gave his girl a minute to compose herself. He reached over and brushed a stray lock of red hair off her face. She didn't even turn to him, just stared at the clubhouse doors. He sighed, and exited the vehicle, heading for her side. When the door was open, he crouched down in front of her and grabbed her hands.

"I'll be right beside you Firecracker," Dagger promised. "No one in there will hurt you or upset you, I'll make sure of it," he promised. She nodded at him and raised her arms to him. He took that as a sign she was ready and lifted her carefully out.

When he reached the door, Navaho was there to hold it open. He had given everyone time to enter first, so the clubhouse was full. Steele greeted him and led him over to the couch. Grateful, Dagger nodded at the VP, and sat holding Zoe on his lap. When he looked around, he noticed the entire club was present, along with the detectives, Mario and

Trent. Preacher stood from his spot at the bar and addressed the room.

"This isn't a hearing or a lynching," Preacher explained, as he looked right at Zoe. "We just want to know why you attacked us, and what was going through your head."

Zoe looked up at him, and Dagger nodded at his girl. She needed to tell her side, and they were all giving her the chance. Not one of his brothers appeared angry at all. They were all relaxed as they waited for her to speak.

"I grew up with Amber pretty much taking care of me," Zoe started. "Our parents died when Amber was eighteen and I was fourteen. She fought hard to get legal custody of me, so I wouldn't have to go into foster care. She quit school, got a job, and moved us into a small apartment. It was hard for her. Amber had to pay for the funeral expenses, sell and clean out our house, and work long hours, but she never once complained. She gave me all the love she had, and we were happy," Zoe explained.

"Amber sent me away to college, and I really hated leaving her. She'd drive up all the time to see me, but I missed her. One day I got a visit from two detectives. They explained that Amber was working for Mario and the club. She had seen something she shouldn't have, and they killed her for it," Zoe whispered.

"Mother fucker," Dagger cursed. Then he watched as Colin stepped forward.

"The two detectives?" Colin asked her. "You were looking for them when you called me."

"Yeah," she admitted. "I was starting to realize that the club wasn't anything like they made it out to be, and I was questioning things. I thought talking to them again would help clear things up."

"You said their names were Candace and Charles?" Colin inquired.

"They were," Zoe confirmed.

"Fuck me," Mario growled. "Candy and Chuck."

Dagger tensed, and Zoe turned to look at him in confusion. The whole room had gone wired, and Dagger felt it was his job to explain.

"We didn't kill your sister," Dagger told her. "The two you met did. Candy was a stripper, and Chuck was a motel owner."

"What?" she gasped in shock. "I don't understand."

"They were stalking my Angel," Mario sadly informed her. "But we didn't know it was them. Amber was helping us figure it out, but they found out. They blackmailed her into helping them instead, then they killed her so she couldn't tell us."

Zoe's head snapped up. "What were they blackmailing her with?" she asked.

"You honey," Mario admitted.

Zoe's face paled, and Dagger immediately pulled her close. When the tears started, all he could do was hold her.

Chapter 29
Zoe

Zoe was heartbroken to find out they blackmailed Amber, and they used her to do it. To think of her poor sister doing whatever they asked just so she would be safe. And it didn't even matter, because they killed her anyway.

"So, I'm the reason she died," she whispered through her tears.

"Fuck no," Dagger roared as he pulled her even closer.

"You had nothing to do with your sister's death," Mario added. "Candy and Chuck would have killed her whether she helped them or not."

"So did your girl survive?" Zoe asked nervously.

She couldn't help smiling when Mario's face seemed to light up. "She's fine honey. We're married now."

"So why were they after her?" she questioned in confusion.

"Apparently Candy had some secret notion that we were meant to be, only I had no idea. When my Angel came into the picture, Candy tried to get rid of her. It didn't go so well," Mario explained.

"So, what does that have to do with my sister?" Zoe frowned.

Mario signed. "Amber was a bartender. We didn't know who the stalker was, only that it was someone that worked at my strip club. We got the employees together, gave them drinks, and Amber helped collect the DNA samples from the glasses. They blackmailed her into switching those samples and setting someone else up as the stalker."

Zoe instantly paled. If her sister was a bartender and worked at the strip club, she wondered if she stripped too. She was paying for two burials and her schooling, she'd need the money.

"What's the matter, Firecracker?" Dagger asked in concern. Zoe looked at him, then turned back to Mario.

"My sister had to strip to pay for my schooling, didn't she?" Zoe asked. She gasped when Mario crouched down in front of her.

"Your sister was hired on to strip. She even got up on stage, but she never went through with it. I saw she was terrified up there, so I gave her a job behind the bar instead. She only ever served drinks. After a bit, I pulled her from the club and she worked for me bartending my parties and meetings. She was a great girl, and I'll never forgive myself for putting her in a position where she was hurt," Mario told her sadly.

"You gave her a job, you didn't make her strip, and you made her life easier. I'll forever be grateful to you for that," Zoe told him. Then something else occurred to her. "Did you fix Amber's grave?"

Mario smiled sadly at her. "It's the least I could do," he confirmed. "She needed to be remembered, and I wanted you to see it and know she was cared for."

Tears ran down her face, and she fell off Dagger's lap and into Mario's arms. He held her carefully.

"It's beautiful," Zoe cried. "The cemetery wouldn't tell me who did it."

"Hey," she heard Dagger yell from behind her. "Go hug your own girl and give me mine back."

Mario chuckled and let her go. She winced as her back pulled when she tried to stand. Immediately, Dagger scooped her up.

"You're going to pull your stitches," he warned. "That means you can't hug anybody else."

"Yeah, that makes sense," Mario chuckled. "You stick with that logic."

"I've got a stick of dynamite in my room and it's got your name on it," Dagger complained.

Mario raised his hands and backed off.

"No more hugging," Dagger grunted as he glared at Mario. "And no more winking," he urged as he glared at Preacher. "Just all of you keep away."

"So, you're claiming her?" Steele questioned.

"She's mine now, she said so," Dagger growled.

"This is great," Dragon grinned. "It's about time you found out what it's like to be jealous."

"I'm not jealous," Dagger huffed. When the room erupted in laughter, Zoe just stared at them all.

"Dagger always gave us shit for being so possessive of our women. It's nice to see he's even worse than us," Dragon explained.

"I like him possessive," Zoe admitted with a small smile. Dagger grinned and pulled her closer.

"She likes me possessive," he repeated.

"Wait," Zoe interrupted. "So where are Chuck and Candy now? Will they come after me," she asked.

"No," Dagger growled. "There's absolutely no chance of that."

"So, they're in jail now?" Zoe pushed.

"Fuck no," Mario huffed. "They went after my girl, and they hurt her. They're in the ground."

Zoe sat there for a second and thought, then she launched herself back into Mario's arms. "You took care of my sister's killers. Thank you."

"What the fuck are you hugging him again for? I just said you can't do that," Dagger yelled. Zoe looked up at Mario to see him grinning at Dagger.

"Fucking Mario," Dagger complained, as he gently pulled her away.

Chapter 30
Dagger

Dagger sat with his girl and knew there was one more thing they definitely needed to figure out. It was time to discuss the knife wound she had suffered. He needed to find out who hurt her, and then he needed to blow the fucker sky high.

"Firecracker?" he asked gently as he placed his finger on her chin and tipped her head up to gain her attention. "Do you have any idea who hurt you?" As soon as he said that, all the brothers went on alert.

"I do," Zoe admitted, and his whole body tensed.

"Tell us," Preacher demanded, as he moved closer to them. "Start where you can."

Zoe looked at Dagger, and he nodded reassuringly at her.

"I had just got back to my apartment. I got out of my car, and as soon as I shut the door, I was grabbed. It was a guy. He lifted me clear off my feet. He was strong, I remember he was so strong. I fought, but it didn't matter. He dragged me into the woods and threw me on the ground. I landed face first, and I landed hard," she told them.

"You didn't see him?" Preacher questioned.

"No," she admitted. "He was behind me the whole time. When I was face down, he came over my back. That's when he stabbed me. It hurt," she whispered. "It hurt so bad."

"But honey," Dragon pushed. "You said you knew who it was."

"I didn't know him," Zoe admitted. "But he had a message for me."

Dagger froze when she turned and looked at him. He stared at the tear that trailed down her cheek. "Tell me," he ordered.

"He said Lisa sent him. I ignored her first message, so she was sending another one, a stronger one," she whispered.

"Mother fucker," Dagger roared. "I went after you. You never once came to me. She should be going after me, not you."

"Umm, you're a badass, I'm not. If I had to choose, I'd pick me too," Zoe informed him.

"She has a point," Lucifer declared.

"No matter what, she'd have to know we'll retaliate," Steele added.

"Yep, but if she's that much of a crazy, she won't think of that. She'll only be thinking of taking out the competition," Dragon told them.

"Shit," Dagger cursed. "What the fuck do we do?"

"We look after her. You claimed her, so she's family now," Preacher immediately stated.

Zoe moved and cried out. Dagger instantly pulled some pain pills out of his pocket. "Time for some meds and a bit of rest," he ordered. He knew her back had been hurting for a while, but his girl was hiding it, so they could get everything worked out.

"Take her to your room, get her settled," Preacher directed. "We'll talk more later."

Dagger nodded, then lifted his Firecracker as gently as he could. He nodded at his brothers and made his way down the hall to his room. When he pushed open the door, he started laughing.

"You like it?" Steele asked from behind him as he looked around too. When Dagger turned, all the brothers were standing there grinning.

Pink toilet paper hung from the ceiling like streamers. Pink flowers were painted on all the walls. Shelves were added to the walls and they were loaded with water guns. Saran Wrap covered the entire opening to the bathroom. But the kicker was the cage in the corner that contained a rooster.

"Fucking bikers," Dagger chuckled, actually happy that he finally got his room done too.

"This is everything I did to the club," Zoe told him in awe.

"Well, at least we aren't keeping it this time," Dagger smirked. "I think I got off easy."

The rooster chose that exact moment to let out its ear-splitting call. Everyone covered their ears, but with Dagger holding Zoe, he couldn't cover his own. When the racket finally stopped, Dagger heard all the brothers laughing. As calmly as he could, he set his Firecracker on the bed. Then he walked over to the shelves and picked the biggest two water guns of them all. The idiots who did this had all of them filled and ready to go. He grinned as he stuck one under each arm and turned back to the brothers. Immediately everyone of them dropped their smiles.

"Don't you fucking dare," Dragon growled.

Dagger let out a roar to rival the rooster, then let loose. Water shot out and soaked the nearest ones, as they turned and tried to trample each other to get out of the way. He emptied them, then grabbed two more as he ran out the door after them.

"You fuckers are going down," Dagger hollered as the bikers ran in all directions and cursed him.

Chapter 31
Zoe

Zoe woke slowly and found several pairs of eyes staring down at her. She quickly closed them, then opened only one this time. The eyes were all still there, and it was unnerving. Sighing, she opened both again and looked around at the faces watching her in curiosity.

"She doesn't look like trouble," one girl sighed.

"She's with Dagger though, she must be trouble," another countered.

"She's got red hair, that's a definite sign," someone else added.

"And she's awake," one of them huffed. "Maybe we could just ask her."

"You trouble?" the first one to speak questioned.

"Apparently," Zoe replied, and they all giggled.

When one girl plopped down on the bed beside her, she studied the girl. The girl seemed to be covered in chalk of some kind, and she was incredibly colourful.

"You're bright," Zoe declared without thinking.

"I like to use pastels," the girl answered with a smile. "I just forget to clean up afterwards. My name's November and we're gonna be the best of friends. The other girls are cool, but you're like my soul sister."

Zoe could only stare at November in fascination. "Why would you think that?" she questioned, then watched as the other girls all started to chuckled.

"You're the pink bandit," one of the other girls explained. "And November here is a giant klutz. The two of you could do some serious damage to this place."

Zoe blinked at the girl, surprised to see she was completely serious.

"I'm Tiffany," the girl continued. She pointed to another girl. "That's Cassie, and the one beside her is Alexandria."

"I'm Zoe," Zoe offered. "But Dagger likes to call me Firecracker."

"I'm Little Mouse," Cassie introduced, "Although I'm not much of a mouse anymore. Tiffany's man calls her Baby Girl, and Alex's man calls her Angel."

"And what about you?" Zoe asked November. November rolled her eyes and smiled.

"The club calls me Klutz, but Jude calls me Rainbow," she told her. "I'm making Dagger build your cabin beside mine," November declared.

"Then I'm making Shadow move ours to the other side of the lake," Tiffany huffed with a frown. "Ours will be way too close to the fall out. Cassie, you should move yours too."

"But I'm four cabins down from you," Cassie giggled. Then she looked at November and lost her smile. "I'll talk to Steele right away."

"Hey," November cried. "I'm not that bad."

"You flooded your cabin last week," Alex laughed with a shake of her head.

"That wasn't my fault," November growled.

"Your tap was dripping, you thought you'd fix it, and the drip turned into you flooding your cabin," Cassie accused.

"I didn't know you had to turn off the water before you took off the tap," November complained as she defended herself.

"Why would you take the tap off when it was just dripping?" Tiffany asked.

"I'm not telling you," November replied as she turned back to Zoe. "So, we've got the cabin location worked out, when's the wedding?"

Zoe choked, and all heads swivelled back to her. "You changed the subject on purpose," she accused November, but the girl just winked. "I don't think Dagger wants a cabin with me. He only just met me."

"Can you stand?" Tiffany asked.

Zoe nodded and carefully rolled off the bed. The girls had already moved to the window, so Zoe followed. When she got there, she blinked at the sight before her. Bikers were wearing tool belts and unloading a ton of wood from a massive truck.

"We didn't bet on this," November complained. "He can't start yet." The other girls nodded in agreement.

As they watched, Dragon ran over to the bikers cursing up a blue storm. "You can't build that cabin next to Lucifer's. You put those two girls together and they'll blow the compound sky high."

"Hey," Lucifer grunted. "My Rainbow's not that bad."

"Catherine let her kitten out the other night, your girl went to find it, and she brought us back a skunk," Dragon growled as he threw up his hands in the air.

"I did do that," November admitted. "I didn't have my glasses on, and I had bits of cotton stuck in my eyes." Then she quickly turned to glare at them all. "Don't ask."

"He's building us a cabin," Zoe announced in awe, as she watched Dagger direct the bikers carrying the wood.

"You're one of us now," Tiffany told her. Then she gave her a gentle hug. Zoe smiled and hugged her back, too happy to reply.

Chapter 32
Dagger

Dagger was excited about starting his cabin. When
the brothers offered to help, he immediately took
them up on it. Zoe had accepted him, and he
couldn't be fucking happier. He knew it was a risk,
putting his cabin next to Lucifer's, but his
Firecracker needed a best friend, and November
was her best choice.

Dagger had woken early and slipped out of bed. He
knew Zoe needed more sleep and he wanted to give
her that. Thank god the brothers had taken pity on
him and returned the rooster to its owner, before
they went to bed. He had cut the Saran Wrap right

down the middle, so Zoe could use the bathroom. All in all, his room wasn't so bad.

Dagger was in the process of framing up the walls when he saw Zoe headed across the lawn. His girl was trailed by November, Alex, Cassie and Tiffany. He smiled when she seemed to only have eyes for him. As soon as she got close, he tagged the back of her neck, and pulled her in tight to his side.

"How's your back this morning?" Dagger asked as he kissed her forehead.

"A bit sore, but I've taken my pain meds, so it should be better soon," Zoe told him.

"I take it the girls explained about the cabins," he questioned as he walked her to a secluded spot near the water. The other girls had headed straight for their own men as soon as they saw them.

Dagger sat and pulled her onto his lap. She snuggled into his neck and leaned into him.

"I hope you don't mind that I've started a cabin for us. You agreed to be mine, so I didn't want to wait," he told her.

"I don't mind at all," she replied with a smile. "With Amber gone, I didn't really know where I wanted to end up. But she's buried here, and I want to be close to her." Then she looked up at him. "And you're here too. I just want to be with you."

He pulled her in tighter and relished the feel of her in his arms. He was glad she didn't argue about the cabin, that would have hurt.

"How long will it take to get the cabin completed?" Zoe asked.

Dagger looked down at her. "If we move at a fast pace, it should be finished in about two or three weeks. We'll have to stay in my room until then."

Zoe just nodded. "I'll need to go get all my stuff from the apartment. And I'll have to tell the landlord I'm moving out."

"We can do that today," Dagger easy agreed. "The sooner we get you settled the better. Do you mind staying in the clubhouse for a while?"

"Not at all," she shrugged. "I was living in a dorm at school, anyway."

"Do you think you might like to finish school?" Dagger asked.

"I don't know," she honestly answered. "I was taking a nursing course, but I couldn't stand it. I didn't realize I hated the site of blood until I started. I was actually trying to figure out a way to tell Amber."

Dagger chuckled. "Well, there are lots of things you can do around here. We have businesses you can work at. Misty always needs help with her photography stuff, and November is an artist. Take some time to figure it out. You don't need to do anything now. Heal and relax a bit."

Zoe smiled at him and nodded. "So, do all the couples have cabins?" she asked.

"Pretty much," Dagger responded. "Mario of course didn't want the average cabin, so he and Alex live in that monstrosity on the cliff," he explained as he pointed it out. "And Preacher wanted to be in the clubhouse, he's not really a cabin type of guy. Him and Macy converted the second floor into a beautiful loft type apartment."

"Wow," she exclaimed. "You all stick together, but have your own space?"

"Yep," he agreed. "Family sticks together, but we have our privacy too. It's kind of perfect."

When his cell rang, he answered without looking at it. "Dagger," he greeted.

"You shouldn't have helped her," Lisa screeched on the other end. "You're mine, and she'll end up destroying you."

Dagger went on alert. "You had someone stab her."

"I did, but she was supposed to bleed out. Then you would have come back to me," Lisa sneered.

"You're delusional," Dagger growled, but she cut him off.

"You get rid of her or I will," Lisa yelled. Then the line went dead.

Chapter 33
Zoe

The next two days were quiet. Zoe spent a lot of time at the lake, sitting by the water with the girls, and watching as Dagger and the other bikers built their cabin. She was floored at how fast the walls went up. Before she knew it, the roof was added, and shingles were being nailed on. It was exciting to watch. She begged Cassie to take pictures so she could make a photo album. Cassie got amazing shots of both the cabin and the guys.

Catherine played in the water, and Misty let Brady paddle around with his friend. Tiffany was starting to show. She was glowing and looked happy. It was a lot of fun, and Zoe didn't feel as alone hanging out with everybody. Dagger also took several breaks to run over and kiss her. Shadow barbecued hamburgers for lunch, and they ate picnic style. Zoe couldn't remember the last time she had this much fun.

When the sun started setting, the guys started packing up their gear. Some of the girls had headed back inside, but Zoe liked staying where Dagger could see her. She knew the knife wound upset him, so she wanted to make things easier by staying close. The injury was finally healing and it didn't hurt nearly as much, but Dagger still worried.

Zoe looked up when Preachers cell rang. The president looked at the screen, scowled and answered. As Zoe watched, Preacher seemed to get angrier and angrier, then his eyes darted to her and then to Dagger. Zoe instantly stood and made her way to Dagger. Something was wrong, and she had to wait until Preacher had hung up to find out what it was. She moved closer when Preacher hung up and pocketed his cell.

"That was Darren," Preacher told the group of bikers that had gathered around. "Zoe's apartment building is on fire."

"Mother fucking Lisa," Dagger growled as he grabbed her hand and started running for the front of the compound.

Zoe glanced back to see tool belts were being dropped, and the bikers that were there were running after them. She tightened her grip on Dagger's hand and tried to keep pace with him. She was short, and her legs weren't as long, so it was difficult for her. Dagger must have realized, because suddenly she was in his arms and he was running even faster.

"Darren and Colin are there, along with the fire department. Watch your speed brothers," Preacher yelled as they all mounted.

Dagger shoved a helmet on her head, strapped her in, and they were on their way. She was surprised to see Dagger's bike was completely surrounded by all the others. It was almost like they expected trouble and were protecting them. It was something she loved and hated at the same time. She clung tighter to Dagger as he took a corner, and he squeezed her leg in reassurance.

When they reached the apartment building, it was pandemonium. The residents were out front, firemen were everywhere, and cops had the area roped off. The bikers ignored them, and they weren't stopped, as they drove around them. As soon as Dagger parked, Zoe was off the bike and running around to the back of the building. She could hear Dagger and the other bikers yelling her name, but she completely disregarded them. Her car was around back, and she had to get to it.

When she got close, she stopped and dropped to the pavement. Just like the building, her car was completely engulfed in flames. The windows were all broken, and the fire was shooting out from all sides. She dropped her head and cried, knowing everything inside was gone. When strong arms surrounded her, she practically collapsed into them.

"We'll replace your stuff," Dagger whispered in her ear. "Everything will be okay."

"No," Zoe cried. "There was a box in the backseat of my car. It had everything I had left of Amber inside."

Dagger sighed and held her tighter. "I'm so sorry Firecracker," he apologized as he kissed the top of her head. The rest of the bikers surrounded them, and just looked at her sympathetically. She knew there wasn't anything they could do.

"Zoe, Dagger," she heard yelled from across the parking lot. She looked up to see one of the boys running towards them.

"Hey Lion," Dagger greeted. "Now's not a good time buddy."

The boy ignored Dagger and crouched down beside her. "Hey Zoe. I saw Lisa and some guy start the fire, they were talking about torching your car, so I got to it before they did."

Zoe whipped her head up and looked at the boy. "The box in the back?" she pleaded frantically.

"It's at the side of the parking lot. I hid it in the trees," he answered with a grin.

As she watched, Dagger nodded at Raid, and the biker took off, but she only had eyes for the boy. She grabbed him and pulled her into her arms, knowing she'd never be able to repay him for what he just did.

Chapter 34
Dagger

Dagger stared at the flames as they shot out of both the car and apartment building. Lisa had gone too far, and this time they could have killed someone. He pulled his Firecracker up off the ground and didn't care in the least that she dragged Lion up with her. He glanced at his brothers and saw they were all just as pissed as he was. When Darren and Colin headed for him, Preacher and Steele moved closer to his side.

"Kid saw Lisa and some guy behind the building. They started the fires," Dagger growled.

"We tried to get footage off the cameras, but the fires too hot. The cameras all melted with the damn tapes inside. The owner's cheap and uses out of date crap," Darren complained.

"You see where Lisa went?" Colin asked Lion.

The kid shook his head. "Sorry, I was too busy hiding and then stashing Zoe's box."

Dagger ruffled the kid's hair. "They could have hurt you."

"Nah," Lion denied with a shrug. "I was careful."

"Isn't it a bit late for you to be running around?" Preacher pushed.

"It's a small town," Lion replied in defence. "Everyone stays out late."

Preacher looked around and scratched his chin. "Don't see any other kids in the crowd watching the fire," he grunted.

"Your family know where you are?" Colin asked.

Lion shook his head, and Zoe pulled him closer. "This is about the fire, not the boy," she angrily reminded them.

"Right, but a kid out by himself worries me," Colin responded.

"He's with us," Dagger piped up. "We'll get him home safe."

When Mario and Trent joined the group, Dagger turned to them in thanks.

"What do you need?" Mario questioned.

"Lion here said Lisa and some guy started the fire. I'm assuming the guy is the same one that hurt my Firecracker. That's twice he's been at this building. Is there any way you can hack into some other cameras and maybe get his picture?" Dagger asked Mario.

"I can," Trent confirmed. "If I can get a picture, I can probably figure out who he is. He's close to Lisa if he's doing this kind of stuff for her. Maybe an old boyfriend, or a cousin or something. I'll go over the file I've already got started on her and try to find something."

"Appreciated," Dagger acknowledged. "I guess there's nothing else we can do here tonight."

"Nope," Darren agreed. "The apartment is basically gone. And you're definitely not suspects, you might as well get gone."

"And quit driving through the barriers," Colin huffed in annoyance.

"Those barriers are just suggestions," Dagger told him, and the brothers chuckled.

Dagger then turned to Mario, as Raid jogged back with Zoe's box in his arms. "Can you take this back to the compound for me?" he asked.

Trent took the box from Raid as Mario answered. "Will do. You want me to take the kid home?"

"Nope," Dagger denied. "I'll do that myself."

Wrench and Raid moved forward. "We'll go with you. Lion can ride with one of us."

"I'm coming too, you need more protection than that," Sniper grunted. "Lisa's stepping up her game."

Dagger nodded as he headed for his bike with his Firecracker. He noticed Wrench got Lion situated on the back of his.

"Head straight back to the clubhouse after," Preacher ordered, as he and the rest of brothers mounted their Harley's.

"Will do," Dagger agreed. Then they were off and following Wrench, who was obviously getting directions from Lion. The kid looked like he was having the time of his life riding on the back of the brother's bike. Dagger chuckled when the kid looked back at him and Zoe, and waved.

When they started driving through the shittiest part of town, Dagger felt Zoe's grip on his waist tighten. He knew she didn't like this, and neither did he. The house Wrench stopped at was horrible. It was small, run down, and the roof actually looked like it was sagging. The lawn was weedy and garbage littered the path to the door. When Dagger looked at Lion, the boy just dropped his head and started up the walk. Before he could move, Zoe was off the back of his Harley and running after him. She caught his shoulder and stopped him.

"Let the men go first," Zoe pleaded. Lion nodded and moved aside. Dagger smiled at the kid in thanks as he moved past them, flanked by Wrench, Raid and Sniper.

Dagger didn't bother with knocking, he pushed open the front door, and stood in shock at the sight that greeted him. He heard his brothers cursing behind him.

"Oh, hell no," his Firecracker roared from behind him.

Chapter 35
Zoe

Zoe stared at the sight before her in disgust. Empty liquor bottles littered every surface, old pizza boxes covered the floor, and dirty clothes were strewn everywhere. The place smelled like a sewer, and Zoe had to cover her nose to stop her stomach from rolling. But it was the sight of the two people going at it on the couch that pissed her off. She pushed the boy behind her and turned her attention to them.

"Hey," Zoe hollered. "Knock that shit off."

Dagger just chuckled at her, but Wrench and Raid moved forward and grabbed the man under the arms, dragging him off the lady. Then Sniper snagged a blanket off the floor and threw it at the woman.

"This your mom and dad?" Dagger questioned Lion.

"She's my mom, but I don't know the guy," the boy told them.

"Mother fucker," the man yelled as he glared at them all. "I paid her fifty bucks to fuck her, and I wasn't fucking done."

Wrench moved forward then and dwarfed the ass. "Get out," he snarled in the man's face.

The man instantly paled and nodded. Without even dressing, he grabbed his clothes and shimmied between the bikers. He was out the door before they could blink. As Zoe watched, Raid moved into the kitchen and started routing through the cupboards and fridge.

"No food," he grunted as he made his way back to them.

Zoe glanced at the woman and noticed she had barely covered herself with the blanket.

"You want a fuck too?" she asked the men with a sultry smile. "I can do you all at once if you want."

Zoe couldn't help it, tears started to run down her cheeks. "Dagger," she whispered in anguish.

Immediately Dagger moved to her side. He turned to the brothers and looked at each of them. Zoe had no idea how they were communicating, but she knew something important was being decided.

"Hey Lion," Dagger called as he turned to him. "How about you and Wrench go pack a bag? Grab anything you want to take with you."

Lion looked at his mother sadly, then nodded and headed down the hall with Wrench. Zoe couldn't take anymore, she moved around Dagger and got close to the mother.

"How can you do this? Your son needs you. Do you even care?" Zoe questioned on a sob.

The woman frowned at her. "I had a good man once, but he left me. Didn't even take our kid. How the hell am I supposed to support us both?" she grumbled as she took a drink from the bottle on the table. "He's old enough to look after himself."

Dagger stepped forward and glared at the woman. "We're taking him with us, and he won't be back," he hissed at her.

Zoe was saddened further when the woman just waved them off. She moved into Dagger and buried her head in his chest. It had been a long night, and this just made it so much worse.

"Think we need to adjust the size of our cabin a bit," Dagger huffed. "Maybe add another bedroom."

Zoe looked up at him in shock. "What are you saying?" she asked.

"Kid belongs with us," Dagger told her.

She threw herself into his arms. "I love you," she cried happily.

"Love you too Firecracker. Now dry your tears before Lion sees them," he ordered.

By the time Lion and Wrench came out, she had herself back under control. She frowned when she saw the small backpack he was carrying.

"That's it?" Zoe asked. When he nodded, she got angry. "We're going shopping tomorrow."

Dagger chuckled. "I like this side of you. All take charge like," he smirked.

She ignored him and turned back to the boy. "Would you like to stay with me and Dagger for a while? You could have your own room at the clubhouse until we finish our cabin," Zoe declared.

He smiled and immediately nodded. "I don't eat much, and I don't need anything new."

Sniper started to chuckle. "The girls will have a field day with you," he declared. "By the end of the week, you won't lack for anything."

They moved towards the door, and Lion headed for Wrench's bike once more. "I want to own a bike one day," he declared.

"We'll get you a dirt bike first," Dagger told him. "Once you have that mastered and you're old enough, we'll move up."

"I'm not coming back here am I?" Lion asked as he looked back at the house.

"No, you're fucking not," Dagger growled as they all started their bikes. "You're a Stone Knight now."

"Awesome," the kid grinned as he held onto Wrench's vest and they took off.

Chapter 36
Dagger

Dagger took Zoe and Lion back to the clubhouse and got them settled. Thankfully, Preacher and the rest of the brothers had no problem with Lion staying with them. Preacher only ordered that they get the lawyer over the next morning and get her to serve his mother with official papers stating she was relinquishing all parental rights to the boy. Dagger thought that was a great idea.

Navaho was in the room next to his, and the brother was kind enough to move to a different room, so Lion could be close to them. Zoe fawned over the boy, but the brothers kept the rest of the girls away. They said the morning was time enough to introduce them all, knowing they'd end up in the clubhouse all night if they met him now.

Dagger gently placed Zoe on the bed, and he was happy to see they stashed her precious box in the corner. She seemed extremely tired, but between the adrenaline, the anguish of worrying over Lion, and her healing wound, it was understandable.

He helped her remove her shoes and pants, then turned as she took off her shirt and bra. He bent at the waist, grabbed the back of his tee and pulled it over his head. Then without turning around, he threw it behind him, grinning when she giggled.

Within seconds they were curled up in bed together, and her warm little body was pressed right against his own.

"What's in the box, Firecracker?" Dagger asked gently.

"It's pictures of my sister, some of her favourite tees, her jewellery, and some little trinkets and things that she really liked. I didn't want to leave it in the apartment, or the storage unit I have. I kind of figured I might need to make a quick getaway, and I didn't want it left behind," she explained.

"Aww Zoe," he sighed as he kissed her head. "I'm so sorry you lost her." He heard her sniff, and it broke his heart.

"When I was told she was killed, it felt like I was dying right along with her. She was all I had left. Even when my parents died, it didn't hurt as much. It's not getting any easier," she admitted.

"Firecracker," Dagger grunted, hating the sadness in her voice.

"But you help," Zoe suddenly blurted, and his body stiffened.

"How's that?" he questioned curiously.

"Just being around you helps. Your support, the way you defended me, your love," she told him. "Then your club accepted me, even after everything I've done. You've given me a new home."

"I love you, Firecracker. I'll give you the world if you let me," Dagger vowed.

"I don't want the world," she huffed as she pushed herself up on his chest. His breath caught as he saw the love she had written all over her face. "I just want you Dagger."

"Damian," he growled. "My names Damian."

"Damian," she repeated with a smile. "It suits you." As he watched, the smile left her face, and a serious expression replaced it.

"Make love to me, Damian," she whispered. "Make me yours."

Dagger looked at her in surprise. "You sure?" he asked.

"If you make love to me and I want to leave later, will you let me?" Zoe was whispered hesitantly.

"Fuck no," he instantly growled. Again, her face lit up in a smile.

"Perfect," she grinned. Then he watched as she sat up and carefully pulled his shirt over her head.

"Jesus Firecracker," Dagger moaned. "You're the only one that's ever been able to render me speechless."

Then he removed the rest of his clothes from his body, as she shimmied her underwear down, and tossed it in the corner. When he returned to the bed, she was already laying in the middle waiting for him.

"Your back?" he asked in concern.

"It doesn't hurt right now, and I know you'll be careful," she whispered.

"Damn straight," Dagger agreed as he covered her body with his own.

He worshipped her body after that. Kissing and caressing every inch of her soft skin. She moaned and writhed beneath him, and he knew she was ready. He entered her slowly and gave her plenty of time to adjust.

"I love you," he told her.

"I love you too," Zoe immediately returned.

They spent the rest of the night making love, and Dagger was in heaven. He knew she was now his everything, his one. When she came, it was his real name she cried, and he soared right along with her. She was his, and she looked at him like she was over the moon about that.

Chapter 37
Dagger

Dagger walked into the common room the next morning with his Firecracker on one side of him, and Lion on the other. Zoe still seemed a bit nervous around all the brothers, but she was getting better. Lion on the other hand beamed as he walked into the room, looking like he was on cloud nine. Every biker they passed on the way to a table greeted them like family. He was proud of the brothers and thrilled that they were accepting of Zoe and Lion without any thought.

As soon as they sat, Navaho showed, and placed heaping plates of pancakes before them. "Eat that up before the rest of the girls arrive, because once they do, all hell's going to break loose," Dagger advised them. He then dug in and was pleased when they did the same. Although Dagger was the only one to finish everything on his plate.

Fifteen minutes later, the rest of the bikers sauntered in with their women. The minute the girls caught sight of Lion, just like he had predicated, all hell broke loose. They squealed, they screamed, and they rushed the poor boy. Dagger would have stepped in, but it looked like Lion loved it. He had probably never been shown any love or affection at home, and that pissed him off.

"So, who gets him?" November suddenly piped up.

Dagger's head snapped up, and he glared at the klutz. "What the fuck do you mean who gets him?" he snarled.

"Well it's obvious he's here to stay, and he's such a sweetheart we all want him," she told him.

"Well fuck that," Dagger grunted as he stood up and moved towards her. "He stays with me and my Firecracker."

Lucifer immediately moved in front of his girl protectively. "Sorry, she wants to bring everything she finds into our house now. The other day she found a baby squirrel and tried to keep it. Let's just say that didn't work out to well."

"What happened?" Zoe asked as she peaked out from behind him.

"It tried to make a nest in one of my boots. Unfortunately, I didn't figure that out until I stuck my foot in it," Lucifer growled.

"Uh oh," Zoe chuckled.

"Yeah, those weren't quite the words I used though," Lucifer grumbled.

"Hey," November interrupted, swatting him on the head. "You didn't have to chuck him across the lawn."

When he turned around, she yelped and ran straight to her brother. Wrench just laughed and tucked his sister under his arm.

More would have been said, but Mario and Trent walked in. Trent had his laptop, and both of them looked serious. When they sat down all the brothers moved to their side.

"I hacked into the camera's and got a picture of the man with Lisa," Trent told them as he brought up a picture on the laptop. "I asked around, searched Lisa's social media, and it looks like he was her neighbour growing up. The guy was infatuated with her, and he followed her around like a puppy dog. He'll pretty much do anything she asks, is what several neighbours told me."

"You know where we can find him?" Dagger pushed.

"Nope," Mario denied. "Apparently the guy has disappeared just like Lisa."

"Shit," Steele cursed. "This is far from over."

"Umm," Trent hedged. "I found something else on her Facebook page."

"Show us," Preacher demanded as he moved forward to join them.

Trent tapped away at his keyboard and brought up the page he wanted. Then he scrolled down until a picture appeared on the screen. Dagger glared at the screen, not believing his eyes.

"Are you wearing a suit?" Zoe asked.

Dagger had only worn a suit once, and that was when his mother had died. Somehow Lisa had gotten the picture and cropped herself in beside him. She was wearing a wedding dress and a tiara. As Trent scrolled further down, he brought another picture up. In this one, he was in his full military uniform, and again Lisa was in a wedding dress and tiara.

"What are the pictures from?" Preacher questioned.

Dagger signed, knowing he needed to tell them the truth. "The first is from my mom's funeral. My dad was a drunk and beat her to death. The second is from the funeral I attended for my platoon. A bomb killed everyone but me." He heard Zoe's tears, and then her arms wrapped around him from behind.

"How the fuck are you so laid back? You crack jokes and keep everything light around here," Dragon asked.

"Exactly, because if I let the darkness in it'll consume me," Dagger admitted.

Then he was shocked as hell, when the entire club stepped forward and closed in. Bodies crashed into him from all sides. Brothers surrounded him, and for once in his life, he felt better.

Chapter 38
Dagger

Once the girls had left, Preacher brought in the lawyer so Dagger could explain what needed to be done. The lawyer was completely on board, and explained that as long as Lion's mother gave up all parental rights to him and his Firecracker, they could start the paperwork to adopt him. The courts would move things along quickly if the mother was going along with it willingly. Dagger wanted to move fast, so the lawyer agreed to have the documents back to them later in the afternoon, so they could get the mother's signature tonight.

Dagger's worry was that the mother would wake up and realize what she was doing. Then she would get greedy and expect the club to give her a shit ton of money for her son. Dagger would pay anything to get that boy away from her, but he didn't want to go that route if he didn't have to.

Dagger thanked Preacher and then headed over to Steele. The brother was hanging out at the bar with Dragon, and the two had their heads together. Dagger knew the brothers were close, and he hated to interrupt. Luckily Dragon saw him approaching and threw him a grin.

"Hey daddy," he greeted. "How you doing with everything?"

Dagger stood behind them and smiled at the brothers. "Surprisingly well. I love Zoe, and Lion's just an added bonus. I think he's going to do really well hanging out with all the bikers."

"I agree," Steele added. "That kids going to be prospecting in no time."

Dagger nodding, completely agreeing. "Wonder if I could borrow your truck for a bit?" he asked.

Steele immediately pulled the keys out of pocket and passed them over. When Dagger went to take them though, Steele didn't let go.

"It comes back in the same condition it goes out in," Steele demanded, before he released them.

Dagger couldn't help but shake his head. "No faith," he grumbled.

He immediately headed for the garage, got the supplies he needed, and loaded up the truck. When he was satisfied with his haul, he grabbed a tarp and covered everything. He didn't need to lose anything on the way. Then he sauntered back to the clubhouse and opened the door. Instead of going right in, he only poked his head in.

"Hey you boring fuckers," Dagger bellowed. When he had all the brother's attention, he smirked. "I'm heading out to do some maintenance on Lisa's house."

Then he didn't wait for a response. He slammed the door and headed for Steele's truck. As he pulled out of the compound, he saw all the brothers racing for their bikes. The roar of Harley's was defeating, and Dagger couldn't be happier. He pushed on the gas and laughed as the brothers tried to keep up with him. A minute later he arrived at Lisa's, and Dagger was out and headed around to the back of the truck. He unhooked the tarp and was pulling out his first item, as the brothers pulled up behind him.

He couldn't help but grin at Navaho, as the brother eyed him suspiciously. "What kind of maintenance do you plan on doing with that?" the brother asked.

Dagger couldn't stop his grin. "Just want to make sure all the leaves are cleaned up," he answered.

"Back the fuck up," Navaho immediately yelled at the brothers. "Fuckers got the tweaked leaf blower."

Dagger ignored him and turned it on. He had to hold it tight, as the force of the wind blew him back a bit. He aimed it at the ground and wasn't surprised when it cleaned up more than the leaves. Grass was torn out and smacked against the side of the house, flowers were ripped from the ground, and Lisa's cute little wicker furniture blew right through the living room window. Satisfied, Dagger turned off the blower and placed it in the back of the truck. Next, he reached for the power washer.

"What's the point of making that fucking mess if you're just going to clean it up?" Sniper asked him, but again Dagger only grinned.

Turing, he walked right past the brothers and headed for the fire hydrant. Once he had it hooked up, he saw the bikers all move to the other side of the street. He ignored them, cranked on his also tweaked power washer, and aimed it at the house. The blast almost knocked him off his feet, but he dug in and leaned forward. It was so strong it actually tore the paint right off the side. Windows blew in, shutters were ripped off, and Dagger couldn't stop the wild roars that came out of his mouth. He was having so much fun.

Chapter 39
Zoe

Zoe and the girls had a blast at the mall. It took four vehicles to get them all there, along with the kids. When they moved as a group from store to store, people actually moved out of their way. It was crazy. Of course, poor Snake and Wrench weren't having much fun, as they had been forced to join them. With Zoe's recent knife wound, and her apartment being burned down, the brothers weren't taking any chances with their safety. Therefore, they had an escort.

They wandered around, and bought Lion clothes, bedding, posters to cover his walls, and every electrical gadget the boy would ever need. Lion looked overwhelmed, but he was grinning the whole time. Cassie surprised them all by paying for everything. Apparently, the girl had a lot of money, and she explained that they were helping her by letting her help him. She had wanted to help with the cabins, but all the guys so far had had enough savings that her money hadn't been needed.

When it looked like Lion was done, they conceded and headed back out to the parking lot. Wrench's phone rang and he hung back a bit to answer it.

"What?" they all heard him bellow at the thing, so they all stopped and looked at the biker curiously. "Why the fuck didn't anyone call me earlier?" Then there was a pause. "We can be there in five," he yelled, as he hung up the phone and started charging towards them.

"Get the fuck in the vehicles," Wrench ordered. "Dagger's at Lisa's, and he's doing some yard work."

Immediately all the girls whooped and headed for the cars, but Zoe just watched them in stunned silence. When November realized she wasn't following, she hurried back and grabbed Zoe's arm. Then the girl started dragging her towards the vehicles.

"Dagger is kind of like you when you were pulling pranks on the club, only on steroids. If he's doing lawn maintenance, that's code for fucking the place up," November explained.

"What?" Zoe asked in confusion.

"You've only seen the relaxed, calm Dagger," Ali told her.

"Now you get to see the crazy, complete nut job side of Dagger," Macy added.

"And you all know this how?" Zoe questioned. Then she sat and listened as the girls told her all about Dagger pretending to be the Marshmallow Man, how he bought a harp for Raid, how he knocked Navaho on his ass with a leaf blower, and how he had a fetish for dynamite. When they pulled up to the house Zoe was completely shell shocked, she had no idea what to expect.

They climbed out of the vehicles, and Zoe could only stare. The grass was completely torn out, there was no paint left on the house at all, windows were smashed, and she could only stare at the roof.

"Is that a mailbox on the roof?" Zoe questioned in awe.

The girls grinned. "It's still standing," Tiffany cheered. "We're not too late."

Suddenly a loud explosion happened, and Zoe instinctively dove to the ground. Leaves and grass rained down, and she covered her head in terror. When the noise stopped, she looked up to find everyone laughing at her.

"Dagger would never do anything to hurt us silly girl," November giggled as she hauled Zoe to her feet.

When the dust settled, she looked to see half the house was gone. She scanned the area and found Dagger grinning like a fool.

"I think I used too much dynamite on that tree I was trying to remove," he chuckled. She heard all the bikers laughing as they approached Dagger and gave him high fives. Then suddenly Darren and Colin were there.

"Can I ask what you're doing?" Colin asked Dagger with a scowl on his face.

"Didn't you hear," Dagger replied in confusion. "I realized the missus needed some lawn work done, and I didn't want to be the neglectful boyfriend. I hurried right over and took care of it before she could get on my case for not doing it."

Colin's mouth dropped open, but Darren just threw back his head and laughed.

"Guess I got a little carried away," Dagger admitted with a shrug. "Think maybe she might not want to see me anymore," he sighed with an exaggerated pout.

As Zoe watched, Dagger headed straight for her, gave her a kiss, then dragged her to his bike.

"That's my new dad," Lion told everyone proudly as he headed for Wrench's bike without even being asked.

Chapter 40
Dagger

Dagger loved when his Firecracker rode on the back of his bike. Her warm body was plastered to his, and it made his heart soar. Three months ago, if a brother would have told him he'd have his one, he would have knocked the fucker out. He couldn't even image not accepting her now.

Despite all that, he was apprehensive about how she would feel about him after what she had seen today. He'd never intended to hide that side of himself from her, but nothing had happened that had made him reveal it. She was a bit of a wildcard herself, but he was just a tad wilder than her. He hoped it didn't cause her to up and leave.

As soon as he entered the compound, he knocked the kickstand down, and helped her off. He carefully removed her helmet, stored it away, then tagged her hand. She watched him, but didn't utter a single word, and that unnerved him. He dragged her to the back of the clubhouse and entered through the door there. It was closer to his room, and he just wanted to get there and talk to her.

As soon as they reached his room, and he had the door shut, he turned to face her. His heart broke when he noticed tears falling from her eyes. He knew he'd lost her, and he had no idea how he would deal with that.

"Firecracker," Dagger whispered, but she raised her hand to stop him from going further.

"No," Zoe sighed. "Let me talk." And all he could do was nod sadly.

"My life hasn't been the easiest, but it was never violent. My sister did everything in her power to keep me fed and in school. I held odd jobs, but she paid for the bulk of it. Then Mario let it slip that she tried stripping to support me. That was hard to hear, but I just thank god she didn't go through with it," she imparted. "That's the craziest thing that's happened." She paused and took a deep breath.

"Your club does violent things to protects its own, and I know that. But to see it in person is a whole different story. You pretty much blew up her house," she whispered.

"No," Dagger denied as he raised his own hand. "I only blew up half her house," he corrected her.

She frowned, and he smartly shut up.

"You love me," she whispered, and his eyes popped open.

"Well ya," he told her. "I thought you already figured that out."

"You blew up a house because she hurt me," Zoe continued.

"Well ya," Dagger stupidly repeated.

"I fucking love you," she practically growled. Then before he could blink, she was running across the room and launching herself at him.

Dagger threw up his arms and caught her, but the momentum knocked him off his feet. He hit the wall and all the stupid water guns hit him in the head before he landed hard on his back. He grunted from the impact as he held his girl tight.

Dagger didn't even get to say anything before his door crashed in and bikers filled the room.

"What the fuck?" Dragon roared as he surveyed the mess.

Dagger couldn't help but grin up at the brother. "She approves of my use of dynamite."

"Jesus," Lucifer cursed. "I was hoping she got pissed and shot you. I haven't won any of the bets yet."

Dagger grabbed the nearest water gun and shot the fucker in the side of the head. "Out," he yelled at the rest of the brothers. "Or you're all next." He grinned when the brothers quickly took off again, shutting the door behind them.

"You like the violence?" Dagger asked her.

"It's kind of fun," she admitted. "Can you teach me how to use dynamite?"

He pulled her down and chuckled. "I said it before, and I'll say it again," he growled. "You were fucking made for me."

She giggled as she peppered his face in kisses. "I love you Damian."

"I love you too Zoe," he growled. "Now get your pretty little ass up, because I'm not making love on the fucking floor."

Zoe grinned as she leaned down and nipped his lip, then jumped up and grabbed a water gun. He growled when water hit him right in the forehead.

"Really?" he smirked.

"Really," she grinned as she shot him again.

"Oh, it's on," Dagger declared as he shot her in the shoulder and jumped to his feet. They made love not long after, but they were both sopping wet when they did.

Chapter 41
Zoe

That evening, Zoe was once again on the back of Dagger's bike. Apparently, while they were having the water gun fight in his room, the lawyer was dropping off the custody papers for Jacob. Dagger had pretty much decided the boy's name was Lion, but until he joined the ranks of the club officially, Zoe was going to continue to call him by his real name.

She always knew she wanted kids, and even though Jacob was older and not technically a kid, she already couldn't imagine her life without him. The boy was strong, kind and extremely loyal.

She glanced to her left, and smiled at Wrench. The biker had insisted on coming too, along with Sniper and Raid. As they told her, Lisa and the man were still out there, and they weren't taking chances with her life. Jacob had been left at Dragon and Ali's cabin, as Catherine had taken an instant liking to him.

Of course, all the bikers were worried that Lisa would step up her game, after what Dagger had done to her house. The whole town was talking about it, and if Lisa hadn't already seen it herself, she would definitely have heard about it.

Trent had also taken down the pics of her and Dagger from her Facebook page and replaced them. Somehow, he had found pictures of her at her worst. The first showed Lisa trashed and puking in a rose bush, and the second showed her in a cat fight with another girl. Both had been captioned 'spinster for life', and had gotten a ton of likes and comments.

Dagger was trying to draw Lisa out, and Zoe was worried it just might work. All attempts to find her had failed, and that was with the club's help, the detectives help, and Mario's help.

As they pulled up to Jacob's mothers house, Zoe began to get nervous. She didn't have any high expectations for this meeting after their last encounter. The lady didn't have any feeling at all for her boy, but she did for her alcohol and money, and that was a dangerous combination.

The bikers placed her behind them, as they headed for the door, and Zoe was perfectly fine with that. She did not want to go in first, afraid of what she could see this time. When Dagger knocked, she hid behind his back. She heard the door open, but Dagger's growl only had her cringing.

"Fucking put some clothes on," Dagger roared, as he pushed inside her house. All three bikers followed, and Zoe was pulled along with them.

"If I would have known you sexy bikers would be showing up here again, I would have got myself all gussied up," the woman purred.

"Jesus, it just gets worse," Wrench complained with barely contained fury.

Zoe finally had a clear view of the woman, and her jaw literally hit the floor. She was dressed in a leather dominatrix outfit, and was carrying a whip. The tiny leather pieces barely covered a thing, and Zoe felt her face flame. Immediately the bikers closed ranks, and Zoe once more found herself looking at their massive backs.

"I was expecting a client," the woman continued. "But I can start with you four."

"Look you nut, I've brought a paper for you to sign, then we'll be out of here," Dagger growled.

"What kind of paper?" she asked, with a bit of bite to her voice.

"It states you're giving up your parental rights to Jacob, and legally signing over his custody to me and my girl Zoe," Dagger explained.

"And what do I get for doing this?" she sneered.

"Your house will remain standing, and I won't be visiting you later with a shit ton of dynamite," he snarled back.

"You took out Lisa's house this morning," she whispered in shock. "I heard about that."

"She pissed me off, just like you're doing now," Dagger grunted.

"I'll sign the paper," she immediately agreed, and Zoe bit her lip to stop from giggling. The other bikers didn't care, and their snickers were loud and clear.

Once the paper was signed, they drove immediately to the lawyer's house. The lawyer promised to file the papers first thing in the morning, and drop off their copy at the clubhouse right after. Zoe couldn't be happier, in under twelve hours Jacob would be officially theirs.

Their cabin was almost finished, and Dagger said Zoe and the girls could go shopping for furnishings soon. Things were coming together, and Zoe couldn't wait to get settled in and begin her new life with him and Jacob.

Chapter 42
Dagger

The next day, Dagger was ready to celebrate. As promised, the lawyer had dropped off the official papers declaring Lion was theirs. He was over the moon and knew his Firecracker was as well. The club had decided to throw a huge barbecue to celebrate, and Navaho, Smoke and Snake had gone shopping for food. The girls were even baking a cake for Lion. Dagger was currently chopping wood for the fire they planned to have later, and Trike was sitting his ass on a log watching.

"You can help you know," Dagger huffed as he brought the ax down and split another log.

"I'm tired," Trike complained. "Brady's getting a tooth and he cries all the time."

Dagger looked at him in astonishment. "Misty's probably just as tired. You mean to tell me you left her with a crying baby."

Trike smirked then, as Dagger stared at him. "No, I dumped him on his Uncle Sniper. I may be tired, but I'm not stupid."

Dagger threw back his head and laughed. "So, Misty's sleeping?"

"Yep, and I'll join her in a bit," Trike smiled.

They both looked up when the roar of motorcycles headed down the road. "Guys must be back from the store," Trike imparted. "Navaho took Steele's truck and the brothers followed. We better help them unload, knowing them, they bought the whole store."

Dagger slammed the ax down into a stump and they headed towards the gate. When they opened and two motorcycles entered, Dagger was surprised to see it wasn't his brothers. They watched as the motorcycles pulled up to the clubhouse and two of the baddest bikers he knew climbed off. They grinned when they saw him.

"Dagger, heard you had a girl. We were driving through and decided to stop by so we could meet her. Preacher told us to come by for the barbecue," Diesel announced in greeting.

Diesel was the president of The Devils Soldiers MC and Hawk was his VP. Their club was made up of ex-military men, and they were some of the best guys Dagger had met. Seeing as he was ex-military as well, he had even considered joining their club before deciding on The Stone Knight's. He spent a lot of time with them when he first got out, and they had been a big help in his transition from soldier to a civilian.

Dagger approached the men and gave them each half hugs and slaps on the back. "It's fucking awesome to see you two. How long are you here for?" he questioned.

"Just the night," Hawk replied. "We're checking on a new girl we got settled about an hour from here and are on the way back."

The Devils Soldiers had a side business where they helped relocate abused women. They got them new ID's, gave them some place to stay, and even set them up with a job. They also set them up with local contacts, someone they could count on if they got into trouble, or the trouble they were running from found them. Even so, the brothers still liked to check on them occasionally themselves. Dagger really admired what they were doing.

"You ready to cross over to our side?" Diesel inquired with a smirk.

"Nah," Dagger denied. "I'm settled here, building a cabin and everything, even adopted a kid."

"Fuck you're all domestic like," Hawk chuckled.

Dagger grinned at the brother, not even trying to deny it. "You two got any women yet?" he asked with a raised brow.

"Nope," Diesel grunted. "I don't have time for it. Club keeps me busy enough."

"It would take a certain kind of girl to put up with us anyway," Hawk added. "We're a little rougher around the edges, not quite the boyfriend type."

Dagger nodded, knowing what they said was true. The guys in their MC had seen some fucked up stuff on their tours, and were in the club for a reason. But they helped women for a living, and the women seemed fine with them.

"The right girl will come around and things will just fall in place," Dagger encouraged.

"Yep," Trike agreed. "Or she'll paint pink flowers on the gates, throw live roosters in the compound, and get little kids to chase you with super soakers."

Both bikers stared at Trike, and Dagger sighed. "I guess you haven't heard how we met. Come inside, we'll have a couple beers, and I'm sure the rest of the brothers will entertain you with stories about my Firecracker," Dagger growled.

The brothers shrugged, grabbed their bags off their bikes and followed them inside. All Dagger could think was that it was going to be a fucking long evening.

Chapter 43
Zoe

Zoe had been introduced to Dagger's two friends and she loved them. They were huge, dangerous looking men, but they were extremely sweet. They made her smile and shocked her at the same time. During the barbecue, the club had filled them in on her antics, and filled her in on Daggers. She had laughed the whole time, and so had the men. She loved the idea that The Devils Soldiers helped women who were being abused. It was an amazing thing to do. Apparently, they were all in the military, and they'd seen their share of abused women.

When they came home, they wanted to help in some way.

When the barbecue was over, the men sat down to have a few drinks. Some of the girls wandered off to feed their babies, or to go for a nap. When she looked over at Jacob, he was sitting with Wrench, but even he looked like he was getting a tad bored.

"Hey Jacob," Zoe called. "Think you'd like to go check out the cabin with me? I hear it's almost done."

He jumped up, instantly excited. "Yes please."

She turned to Dagger, wanting his okay first.

"Go ahead honey. We'll probably clean up first," he told her as he moved towards her and kissed her head.

"I'd love to see the cabins," Hawk interrupted. "I'm building one and maybe I could steal some ideas from you guys."

"Sounds good to me too," Diesel added. "Give us about ten and we'll be right behind you."

Zoe smiled and nodded, then Jacob took her hand and dragged her off.

"Lion," Dagger called before they got too far. "Keep an eye on my Firecracker. She gets into trouble easily."

"Yes sir," Jacob grinned, and she glared at Dagger.

"What trouble can I possibly get into down there?" she yelled in annoyance as she kept walking.

"I don't want a fucking pink cabin," he yelled back.

Zoe flipped him the bird, and she could hear his laughter as they walked away. It was beautiful out and Zoe loved the walk. Jacob talked her ear off the whole way. He told her about the dirt bike him and Dagger were looking at. He told her about the motorcycle Wrench was letting him help fix. And he told her about the breakfast Navaho had taught him to make. The kid was a sponge, and he was taking full advantage of it.

The cabin looked done from the outside, but the inside still needed a bit of work. The walls were painted and the kitchen was in, although it looked like the plumbing still needed to be hooked up. The ceramic tile was installed in both the bathrooms and the kitchen, but the wood flooring was still piled up in boxes in the corner. There was a beautiful stone fireplace in the living room, but the unit itself had to be placed inside. All in all, it looked good, and Zoe was thrilled with all the work Dagger and the club had accomplished.

"Can we move in soon?" Jacob asked.

"I think so," Zoe replied with a smile. "It looks like it won't be long now."

They exited the cabin and walked around to the front of it. The ground had been torn up, but it would be perfect with some wildflowers growing there. Dagger said he'd put some sod down and make it look nice again.

"Whose boat is that at our dock?" Jacob questioned, and she looked towards it. "I didn't think Dagger had bought one yet."

"He hasn't," Zoe told him as she studied it. It was a small motorboat, and it was one she hadn't seen before.

She moved closer, when two people suddenly stepped out from the trees. She knew right away it was Lisa and the man that had stabbed her. Both held guns, and both had them pointed at her.

Zoe turned towards Jacob and gave him a shove in the direction of the clubhouse. "Run," she screamed. Then she ran straight at the couple. They looked at her in complete shock, and she used that distraction to knock them both to the ground. They rolled for a minute, and then she found herself knocked to the side with Lisa was standing over her.

"He got away," the man grunted in frustration. "I would have had him if she hadn't tackled us."

Then he walked over and grabbed her arm, roughly pulling her to her feet. Zoe tried to free herself, but his grip was too strong.

"Let's go for a short boat ride," Lisa ordered as she pulled a zip tie from her pocket. The man yanked

Zoe's hands behind her back and then bound them together.

As they dragged her to the boat, she prayed Dagger was close. Jacob was fast, but she had no idea how Dagger would catch a boat.

Chapter 44
Dagger

Diesel and Hawk helped Dagger move the picnic tables back closer to the side of the clubhouse. They kept them out of the way and only got them out when they needed them. The barbecue had been a huge success, and Dagger had enjoyed having his Firecracker and Lion there with him. It had just made it that much more special.

When they were done, the three of them started across the property. The cabins were quite far, but the men enjoyed the walk. Diesel and Hawk ran their club differently. Because the men had all been in the military, they had shared close quarters.

Because of that most preferred to purchase homes of their own, away from the compound. They still had rooms that they could use if the need arose, but they enjoyed their separation. Dagger could understand that. It was difficult to sleep in a small space with a dozen other men, and he hadn't enjoyed that experience at all. Even so, he still preferred being close to his brothers. It was something he needed.

They were about halfway there when Diesel stopped and peered ahead of him. "That the kid running this way?" he questioned.

Dagger looked in the distance, and sure enough Lion was barreling flat out towards them. Immediately Dagger got an uneasy feeling. The kid wouldn't leave Zoe alone unless something was wrong. He started walking faster in Lion's direction, and then he cursed and picked up speed when he heard Lion bellow his name. He could hear the other two bikers pounding after him.

Lion was out of breath when he reached them, and he leaned way over to drop his hands to his knees. The boy was out of breath, but it was the tears streaming down his face that had Dagger terrified.

"They got Zoe," Lion panted.

Dagger's whole body locked solid. "Who got Zoe?" he thundered.

"Lisa and the man that stabbed her," Lion told him.

"How the fuck did they get in?" Diesel questioned. "This fucking compound is locked tight."

"Boat," Lion explained. "They came in on a boat."

"How did you get away?" Hawk asked as he narrowed his eyes.

"Zoe tackled them and told me to run. They had a gun, but she took them by surprise. They didn't shoot her, I would have heard the shot," Lion told them.

"Mother fucker," Dagger cursed. "Run to the clubhouse and tell the brothers. I"m going after her."

Lion nodded and took off once more, his exhaustion forgotten. Dagger was relieved Lion was unhurt, but he was scared to death of what those two would do to his Firecracker. He turned back to the cabins and ran as fast as he could for the lake. He didn't have to look back to know Diesel and Hawk stayed with him. When he reached the bank, he could see a boat in the distance. He could just make out Lisa and the man with her, but there was no sign of Zoe.

"Hey," Lucifer yelled from his dock. "Move your ass."

Dagger swung his head Lucifer's way and saw the brother was in a small motor boat with Klutz at his side. Dagger flew across the ground and pounded down the dock. With one leap he was in the boat too. Then he was knocked on his ass as the other two bikers landed on him.

"Sorry," Hawk growled. "But there's no fucking way we're being left out."

The boat rocked as they all got settled. Then they were moving in the water, heading after his girl.

"Does this thing go any faster?" Dagger growled as the other boat got further and further away.

"Fuck no," Lucifer complained. "It a goddamned fishing boat. It's not meant for high speeds."

Suddenly a roar sounded from just up the lake, and a boat unlike any Dagger had ever seen flew around a bend and headed straight for them. The thing was twice the size of theirs and about five times as fast. He grinned as he watched Mario pull up beside him.

"I saw what happened from my deck. Get the fuck in and let's go," Mario ordered.

Dagger shook his head and jumped from Lucifer's boat to Mario's. Once more he was knocked off his feet as Diesel and Hawk followed. Klutz was already in the air when Lucifer caught her around the waist.

"Oh no you don't," he roared. "They don't need the added weight."

Dagger barely heard Klutz arguing about him calling her fat before Mario shoved the throttle down and roared away. He grabbed onto the side and held on for dear life as the boat shot through the water. He leaned sideways and peered out the front, then his heart stopped as he saw his Firecracker thrown from the boat, but it was cinder block that was attached to her leg that freaked him out even more.

Chapter 45
Zoe

Zoe screamed and struggled as they dragged her down the dock. The man who had stabbed her let go of her, turned, and then struck her in the jaw with his fist. She saw black spots and would have gone down again if he hadn't been holding her so tight.

"That little shit ran," Lisa hissed. "We need to move before we have the whole goddamn MC after us."

Lisa was almost at the end of the dock, and the man dragged Zoe along with him. She continued to pull and hit him, but it did nothing. Panicking, she screamed, and received another back hand for her efforts.

"Shut up before I tell him to knock you out," Lisa complained as she walked down the dock.

Zoe stared at the boat in horror. She knew if she got in it the bikers probably wouldn't be able to find her. She also knew if she fought, she'd be hit again. If she didn't fight, at least she'd be awake to make another escape attempt. If she was out, she wouldn't be able to do a thing. Zoe cringed as she was shoved hard. She turned and glared at the man, but he simply smirked at her.

Lisa got in first and kept the gun trained on her. Carefully Zoe climbed in, and the man followed. As soon as she sat down her arms were grabbed and pushed together. She could barely blink before they placed a zip tie on them and pulled tight. She cried out from the pain it caused, pulling a laugh from Lisa.

"You could have stepped aside you know. I had our whole life planned, but you couldn't do that," Lisa sneered.

Zoe gaped, not understanding how the girl could be so dense. Then she was jostled as the boat powered up and started to move through the water.

"I had the wedding shower planned already, and the guests invited. It was going to be the talk of the town," Lisa continued. "I was planning on putting our cabin up by Mario's. I didn't want to be too close to Tripp. You know he's not a very nice man."

"He was a cop," Zoe admitted with a frown. "He's one of the best men I know."

"Well he's dating a girl that should have been born in the sixties. Someone needs to tell her the hippy look is out," Lisa scowled.

"She dresses like a gypsy, not a hippy," Zoe defended. "And she's a friend of mine."

Lisa kept talking, but Zoe tuned her out. She'd heard enough and she wanted to concentrate on the shore. She was sure she'd glimpsed November running for her cabin. As they got further away, she realized she was right, November and Lucifer were climbing in another boat. She would have kept looking, but the man knocked her off the seat, and she landed hard in the boat's bottom. She had no idea how long she laid there for, when a chain was suddenly wrapped around her ankles.

"What are you doing?" Zoe cried fearfully.

"We stole a cinder block from a pile by the cabins. We're tying it to your ankles," Lisa declared with a grin. "You won't die if we throw you in and you swim away."

Zoe could only stare at the girl in horror. When she leaned up a bit and looked at her ankles. She saw that in fact the chain was wrapped tight around them. With her hands tied there was no way she could get it off. She heard a loud motor, but couldn't see anything while laying in the boat. All she could do was pray that help was on the way.

The motor was getting closer, but Lisa must have decided they were far enough out, because she nodded to the man. He grunted and struggled to lift the block up onto the side of the boat. At the same time Lisa yanked Zoe to her feet. She only had a minute to take a deep breath before they shoved the cinder block over the side, and she followed.

Zoe hit the water hard and was immediately dragged down. She couldn't struggle and she couldn't fight. All she could do was stare up as the surface got further and further away. It only took a minute for the block to hit the bottom, and when it did, a cloud of dirt swirled around her. She held her breath as long as she could, but it burned. Her body demanded air. Soon she'd have to take a breath, and she prayed November and Lucifer reached her before then.

Chapter 46
Dagger

Dagger was freaking out. Seeing his Firecracker thrown from the boat terrified him. Mario was gaining on them, but every second meant the difference between life and death.

"Move this fucking boat," Dagger bellowed.

He wanted to jump in, but he knew they weren't close enough. Then a gun fired and they were all forced to duck for cover. It hit the side of the boat and Mario actually growled. When he looked up, he saw it was the ass that stabbed his girl. Before he

could fire again, Dagger watched in surprise as a
bullet tore through the ass's shoulder. The gun
instantly dropped, and the man went flying
backwards. Dagger turned to see Diesel holding a
gun, and it was still trained on the other boat.

"Excellent shot," Hawk grinned, pounding his prez
on the back. "Now you and the suit need to contain
those two idiots while we go save the girl."

Dagger didn't waste any time. He dove right into
the water and forced his body down. The weight of
the wet boots and leather helped him reach the
bottom, and he was fucking grateful. It was murky
and hard to see, as he sunk lower and lower. Then
he saw her. She was holding her breath and twisting
in the water. Her wrists were tied, and the chain
attached to her legs held the cinder block. He
pushed through the water and came upright beside
her. His heart broke as he locked eyes on her
frantic ones.

Dagger went straight for the chains and tugged, but
they didn't give. He tried unwrapping them, but
there was just too much of them. Then Hawk
appeared beside him. The two worked side by side,
but it was impossible in the murky water to

accomplish much. Suddenly Hawk hit him in the shoulder and pointed to his girl. She was floating in the water now and all the fight was gone out of her. Dagger knew immediately she was dying, and it felt like his world was stopping. He only had a minute left himself before he would need to take a breath.

Hawk swam lower and grabbed the side of the cinder block and made a lifting motion. Dagger immediately caught on, swimming to the other side and lifting as well. The damn thing was heavy, but it moved. Taking that as a good sign, he put everything he had in lifting it. Both he and Hawk planted their feet in the mud and pushed. It worked, they actually made headway and started to move to the surface.

They were about a third of the way up, when Lucifer appeared beside him. He pushed Dagger out of the way and grabbed the block himself, motioning to Zoe. Dagger nodded, let go, and moved for his girl. She was swaying in the water now and floating up with the block. He was absolutely terrified that they were too late. He tagged her around the waist, brought her in close to his body, and shot up. It put all his water training from his time in the military to use, and he was grateful to have Hawk by his side.

They were almost to the top when about eight bodies dropped into the water all around him. Hands grabbed his arms and pulled, but thankfully nobody tried to take his girl from him. More moved to help Hawk and Lucifer with the block. The fucking thing weighed a goddamned ton, and Dagger had no idea how it didn't go through the bottom of the damn boat.

When he broke the surface even more arms were there, and they lifted him from the water, and hauled him quickly into Mario's boat. Zoe was pulled from his arms and he knew enough to let go. His brothers were there now, and they'd do everything to save her. He struggled to reach her and found Raid already starting CPR. Shadow was pushing on her chest while Sniper was breathing air into her mouth. He would have protested, but he was just too tired. Dragon and Wrench were at her legs and they were finally getting her free of the chains. All he could do though was stare at her chest. It wasn't fucking moving.

The brothers didn't give up though, and Dagger moved closer, getting as near as he could to her head. Leaning down he did the only thing he could, he pleaded with her.

"Zoe baby, I need you to fight. I've just found you, and I'm not living my fucking life without you. You need to wake up now and come back to me baby. I've never needed anything before, but I fucking need you," he growled.

Suddenly she started choking, and the brothers quickly flipped her to her side. Dagger grabbed her head, and angled it so it was off the seat. When she started throwing up water, it fell harmlessly to the bottom of the boat.

"That's it honey," Dagger cried in relief. "Let it all come out."

Then he eyed each of his brothers and nodded, silently thanking every single fucking one.

Chapter 47
November

November was on the front lawn hosing down the clothes she had worn when doing her pastels. She found it easier to get them clean if she did this first. She'd ruined several outfits in the past by throwing them all in the washing machine together and had learned her lesson. Jude was inside, and he was changing before heading back up to the clubhouse. Of course, it had been her fault he had to do that. She had bitten into her burger and the ketchup had squirted out and hit him in the chest. She had found it pretty funny, but he hadn't.

November glanced up when she saw Zoe and Jacob checking out the progress on their cabin. She couldn't wait until they moved in. It was going to be so much fun. She turned off the hose, rung out her clothes, and was headed back in when she heard the screaming. It looked like Zoe was tackling two people while Jacob took off in the direction of the clubhouse. Then one of the people stood and held a gun on her new friend. Freaked, November dropped her clothes and ran for the front door of her cabin. She would have yelled for Jude, but she didn't want to draw attention to herself.

November practically ran through the door in her haste to get inside. She darted through the living room and headed straight for the bedroom, just as Jude was coming out. They collided, and she would have gone down if he hadn't caught her.

"Jesus, Rainbow, what's the hurry," Jude questioned in concern.

"Two people have a gun and they've got Zoe down by the water. Jacob got away and he's headed for the clubhouse," she hurried to tell him.

As November watched, Jude cursed, then moved to the nightstand where he kept his own gun. Next, he snagged his cell as he headed for the porch. They were just in time to see a boat taking off from the dock, then he had his cell at his ear.

"Zoe just got kidnapped," Jude growled, getting right to the point. "Lisa and the ass threw her in a boat and took off. I'm going after them, but you need to get everybody down here now."

Then he hung up and took off for their own boat. When he jumped in, November was right on his heels. He glanced at her to make sure she was sitting before he cranked the motor and took off. All she could do was hold on for the ride. The next few minutes were a blur as Jude collected Dagger, Hawk and Diesel from another dock and then ended passing them off to Mario, who came out of nowhere.

When they reached the boats again, the club was right behind them in more boats. Some jumped in the water, and some moved to secure Lisa and her now bleeding companion. November watched in horror as they pulled Zoe out of the water with no pulse. As they were working on her, Trike and

Tripp were removing a huge chain and cinder block from her legs. As she watched they moved it to the boat holding Lisa and the man, along with Shadow and Snake.

November glanced at all the boats, but nobody was watching her, and Jude was just climbing out of the water. The boats were close together, so with all the bikers moving around, nobody noticed when she climbed from her boat to Mario's. She hurried across the deck, then carefully climbed into Lisa's boat. Neither Shadow nor Snake saw her, and both Lisa and the man were tied up and gagged.

November moved quickly to the cinder block and the chains. Grabbing the chains, she hurried over to Lisa and began tying them to her legs. The girl started thrashing, but with the gag she couldn't scream, and all the bikers were busy watching the commotion as Raid and Dagger tried to breathe life back in Zoe. The cinder block was already on the seat, so once she had the chain secured, she leaned on the seat and used her feet to shove it over the side. The splash it made was loud, and the chain immediately started to follow. She hurried to Lisa and grabbed her arm, hauling the girl to her feet. The bikers were just turning in her direction when the chain yanked Lisa out of the boat. She hit the water with a scream that was heard even through the gag.

"Woman overboard," November shouted happily as everyone stared at her in shock. She caught Zoe's eyes as the girl leaned over and threw up water in the bottom of the boat and winked at her.

Chapter 48
Dagger

Dagger's heart started beating again right along with his Firecrackers when she took a breath. When she'd starting throwing up, Raid was right by his side giving him instructions.

"Keep her tipped over so she doesn't swallow it again. She needs to get every bit of lake water she can out," Raid explained.

Dagger ignored the brothers surrounding him who were climbing back into the boats and dumping out wet boots. He also avoided looking at the boat that held Lisa and her minion. He was worried if he got a glance at either of them, he'd pull out his gun and shoot them. It was safer to focus completely on his girl. When there was no sign that she would throw anything else up, Dagger lifted her and sat with her in his lap. There was no way in hell he was letting her go.

"Dagger," Zoe whispered hoarsely as he pulled her closer. "You got to me in time."

"I'll always get to you in time. But how about if you don't accept rides from killers anymore," he teased.

She actually smiled, and his heart soared. His girl was going to be just fine. A blanket was thrown over them, and Dagger made sure Zoe was completely covered. She was shaking from the cold.

"She'll be okay," Raid assured him. "It looks like she could use a bit of ice on her jaw, but other than that she just needs a hot shower and lots of rest. Although you'll still want Doc to check her out as well."

Dagger was about to answer, when a scream and a loud splash came from one of the boats. His head shot up and he was just in time to see Lisa hit the water with a chain wrapped around her legs. When he looked at November, she yelled 'woman overboard', and then grinned.

"Jesus," Diesel grunted. "I think she just took care of Lisa for you."

"My wife's a klutz," Lucifer smirked as he started climbing across all the boats to reach her. When he did, he kissed her cheek and pulled her close. "Now dear," Lucifer teased with a smirk, "you know you need to be more careful."

Wrench, who was wringing out his tee, threw back his head and laughed, then every biker there joined in.

"I guess we're not going in after her," Hawk grinned.

"Fuck no," Dagger replied. "Although I think we need to mark the spot with a buoy or something so we can clean the mess up later."

"I got it covered," Mario replied, as he did exactly that. "I'll send some men out here later tonight to get rid of the body."

Zoe sat there, and Dagger knew from her silence that she didn't care one bit what happened to Lisa. But when she looked at November, she started crying.

"You killed someone for me. You're the best friend ever," Zoe sobbed. Then of course November started crying too.

"You're my best friend too, I didn't actually trip," she wailed as she rocked all the boats trying to climb across them all and get to his girl. The brothers cursed and grabbed onto the sides, and Lucifer attempted unsuccessfully to catch her.

"Jesus Christ," Lucifer growled. "You're going to send all of us into the water again."

But November made it to Zoe, and Dagger found his girl yanked from his arms. Then the two of them curled up together and cried some more.

"Think we can go to shore now before we all end up with pneumonia," Dragon grunted. The men all nodded in agreement, then stepped into different boats so they were evenly distributed.

"Sorry honey, but I really want my girl back," Dagger told Klutz, as he retrieved Zoe and placed her back on his lap.

The boats started moving, and his Firecracker curled in and went to sleep. Raid assured him that was okay, and he breathed a sigh of relief.

"I see why you don't want to come join our club," Diesel chuckled. "Ours is pretty tame compared to yours."

"You ass," Hawk complained with a scowl. "Now you just jinxed us, and I hope like hell the mess you just asked for lands in your lap first."

Dagger chucked as Diesel scowled right back at his VP. "Not going to happen."

"Oh, it's going to happen," Dagger snickered. "And it's going to be the best thing to ever happen to you."

Chapter 49
Zoe

Zoe woke in Dagger's bed at the clubhouse. Apparently, she had passed out on the boat ride back. Dagger was curled up around her, and when she looked around the room, she found Jacob sitting on the floor watching her. She tried to move, but the arms wrapped around her tightened.

"Not ready to let you go yet," Dagger growled.

"Jacob," Zoe pleaded, and Dagger sighed then released her.

She carefully climbed over Dagger and rolled to the side of the bed. Jacob watched her, and she saw tears streaming down his face. She opened her arms, and he jumped up and flew into them.

"I'm okay," she soothed him.

"I left you," Jacob cried, and she could feel his body shaking.

"I know honey, and because of that we're both alive. You got to Dagger and he got to me in time," Zoe told him.

"I shouldn't have left you," he choked out as he leaned back and swiped at the tears.

"And if you hadn't, we'd both be at the bottom of the lake and no one would have known. You did the right thing, and you did what I asked. I knew you were safe, that was a huge relief," Zoe explained.

Jacob thought a minute and finally nodded. Zoe couldn't help smiling at him. "It's over now. The house will be done soon, we'll move in and be a family."

"We're already a family," Jacob told her. "Dagger said he got the papers from my mom."

"You're right," she grinned. "I also heard he bought you the dirt bike."

Jacob's smile got wider. "Yeah, it's awesome."

"You'll have to let me watch when you ride it," Zoe encouraged.

"You got it," he promised. Then he climbed to his feet and headed for the door. "I'm going to go find Wrench. I'm super glad you're okay."

When he was gone Dagger pulled her close again, and she found herself sprawled across his chest. She leaned down and buried her face in his neck. She wasn't taking anything for granted anymore.

"I love you, Damian," she whispered.

"I love you too Zoe," he immediately returned. "You scared the absolute shit out of me."

"I'm sorry," Zoe apologized. "I scared the shit out of me too. But it's over, right?"

"Your best friends with November, it will never be over," he chuckled before turning serious. "Doc checked you out when we got back. You'll need some rest, but you'll be good."

"So how long until the cabin's ready?" she asked to change the subject.

"I have something to take care of first, but I'll get the guys to help so we can be moved in by the end of the week," Dagger promised.

"That sounds perfect," she grinned. "What do you have to take care of?" He sighed, and she frowned. "You're going to do something to Lisa's friend."

"I am," Dagger admitted. "He hurt you, and he needs to know what it feels like."

Zoe nodded, knowing Dagger needed this.

"You're not going to argue about this?" Dagger questioned her with surprise.

"No," she shrugged. "I understand. But come see me afterwards, I'll make sure to let you know just how alive I am."

Dagger smirked and her heart stopped. "You got it Firecracker. And just so you know, I'm going to wait a little while, then I'm going to ask you to marry me. We just need more time so you can get completely comfortable with me, but you're going to say yes when I do."

"I don't need time to get comfortable with you," Zoe immediately complained. "I know all I need to know."

"You saying you'll marry me now?" Dagger asked with obvious surprise.

"Dagger, I love you. I lost my sister. I was stabbed. And I was thrown in a lake with a brick tied to my legs. I've learned life is too short. You find something that you love you go all in, and that's what I intend to do. I'll marry you today if you want," she grinned. Then she leaned down and kissed him.

Dagger kissed her back, then she found herself flipped on the bed and his warm body pressing her down into the mattress. He reached across her, pulled open the nightstand drawer, and grabbed a small pink box. He laid it on her chest, opened it, and pulled out a ring.

"I had this made for you a couple days ago. It's a traditional diamond, but I surrounded it in pink stones to remind you I'll always think of you as my little pink bandit," he told her. Then he lifted her hand and slid the ring on her finger. She stared at it as tears ran down her face.

"It's beautiful," Zoe hiccuped.

"I'll give you two days, then you're officially mine," Dagger declared.

"Perfect," she agreed. Then they spent the rest of the day talking quietly and making plans. For the first time since she had been told her sister was dead, she was looking forward to the future.

Chapter 50
Dagger

Dagger waited until his girl fell asleep to head into the common room and gather the brothers. As soon as he stepped into the room, conversation stopped and heads turned his way. Diesel and Hawk had already taken off. Apparently, they were late in picking up the girl they were relocating, and needed to move out. Dagger had gotten to say his goodbyes, and he made it clear to them he owed them.

Navaho was the first to approach. "You ready for some fun?" he questioned.

"It's definitely time to let off some steam," Dagger agreed.

"Snake and Smoke have already got him chained up in the shed," Navaho informed him.

Dagger nodded his thanks and headed in that direction. Of course, as soon as he moved chairs were shoved back and he had a small entourage. He turned to see Steele, Dragon, Trike and Shadow at his back, along with Navaho. He didn't acknowledge them, just kept moving. Dagger already knew Mario had Trent and a couple of his men fish Lisa out of the water. What they did with her, he had no idea, and frankly he didn't care.

When he reached the shed, Snake opened the door and he stepped inside. It was then Dagger got his first look at the moron who helped Lisa. He looked absolutely pathetic. He hung from the chains and was dressed only in a pair of jeans. The brothers had already stripped him of everything else. He glared at the man, who he was recently told was named Brad.

"Brad," Dagger sneered, hating that name. "What the fuck would ever make you think siding with Lisa was a good thing?"

"I love her," the moron instantly replied, but he looked unsure of his answer as he eyed them all warily.

"Is that the excuse you're going to use, to explain stabbing my girl in the back and tying a cinder block to her leg?" Dagger growled.

Brad leaned back and paled. "Lisa promised we'd go away together once Zoe was taken care of."

"Lisa wanted Zoe out of the way so she could have me for herself," he sneered. "How the fuck long have you been panting after her?"

Brad instantly glared. "I haven't been panting after her. We've been in an on again off again relationship."

Dragon threw up his hands. "You going to fuck him up, or stand here and chit chat?"

Dagger grinned. "This is great, but I'm not really digging the shed."

Dragon narrowed his eyes at him. "What do you have in mind?"

"Care to drag his ass out of here and take him out in the yard," Dagger questioned.

All the brothers grinned and moved forward, and the moron started pleading. Of course, he was ignored as the chains were unhooked and they dragged the man out. Dagger led the way to the clearing he had set up earlier. It was dusk now and starting to get dark, so this would be perfect. The brothers stopped when they saw the stakes pounded in the ground.

"Chain him face up," Dagger instructed with a smirk. He moved to a box and dragged it over while the brothers got the moron situated. When they were done, they stepped back.

"Do you know what I call my girl?" Dagger asked the moron as he got close. The man was shaking in fear as he shook his head.

"I call her Firecracker," he explained. "You see, I kind of have a thing for blowing shit up."

Then he moved to the box and pulled out three large firecrackers. "It's a beautiful night," Dagger grinned. "Perfect for a show."

Then he walked over, jabbed one between the moron's legs, and the others under each arm pit. He had made sure the stakes were close, so his arms and legs were pulled in tight to his body. The firecrackers stood up perfectly. He then pulled a lighter out of his pocket.

"Jesus, you're crazy," the moron yelled, and Dagger just smirked at him. He could hear the brothers chuckling behind him.

"We've been saying that for years," Steele felt the need to reply.

Dagger lit the fuses and moved out the way. The moron screamed as the firecrackers rained sparks on him and burned his skin, before they shot out and lit the sky in a blaze of colour. The doors to the clubhouse were thrown open and brothers piled out. Dagger continued the show for another half hour, and the moron got quieter and quieter. By the time he was done, the brothers were cheering and the moron was a charred mess. Thankfully the woman had all been kept away.

Dagger approached the moron once he was out of firecrackers. "You shouldn't have hurt my woman," he growled. Then he pulled a knife from his back pocket, switched it open, and drove it through the man's heart.

"Well, that was certainly a different way to go," Trike announced, and the brothers all laughed.

Chapter 51
Zoe

Zoe didn't see much of Dagger over the next two days. He was working hard, with help from a lot of the other bikers, to get the cabin finished. Even Jacob was put to work, and it looked like he really enjoyed it. He was fitting in wonderfully with the bikers, and Zoe couldn't be happier. With the men busy and the danger over, this meant the girls got to go shopping. Zoe spent one full day buying things for the cabin and she was over the moon. She had a huge entourage too, and they made it so much fun.

She kept the colours pretty neutral, but then threw in splashes of reds and golds in accessories. Every girl explained that most of them took their bedroom decorations with them, but Zoe wasn't too sure about that. She was against using pink anywhere in the cabin too. She did keep the water guns though, remembering how their last water gun fight ended up.

Zoe also got to go wedding dress shopping. She tried on about fifty dresses, amusing all the girls by trying on every dress they suggested. Of course, they each had their own tastes. Fable picked out an old-fashioned dress with capped sleeves, Macy picked out a simple short sundress, Alex picked out a huge lacy ball gown, and November picked out a red dress. Zoe had nothing to say to November, and just stared at the red dress in shock. That girl was always surprising her.

In the end, she picked out a long simple white dress. It had an empire waist, a heart neckline and it was strapless. The skirt fell to the floor and was covered in a fine lace. As soon as she put it on, she knew it was the one. When Zoe walked out of the dressing room, no one said a word, then they all started crying. It was emotional, it was fun, and it was exactly what she hoped it would be. The only thing missing was her sister. It broke her heart that her sister wasn't with her, she would have loved to have been a part of this.

They were all headed back, when the girls took her on a detour. When they stopped in front of a tattoo shop, Zoe was confused. It was then explained to her that they had started a tradition where they got a tattoo with their man's name and a picture that symbolized their nickname. Macy was the first to pull up her sleeve and show hers. It was stunning. It had Preacher's name and above that was a small, delicate looking hummingbird. Zoe got chills thinking about having Dagger's name tattooed on her.

"Will you do it?" Ali asked her.

"I think this is perfect," Zoe told them. "I could get a stick of dynamite with his name."

"It is fitting," Tiffany admitted with a grin. Then all the girls took a minute to show her theirs. By the time they were done, Zoe was excited to get hers done.

When she stepped into the tattoo parlour, she asked if they had time for her to get two done. They said yes, so she got her tattoo for Dagger, but she also got a small butterfly tattoo on her wrist. Under it she had them put Amber's name. She wanted to do something that would keep her sister close, and this seemed perfect. When the girls saw it, they started crying again, so when they got back to the compound, they were all a blubbering mess. Tools were thrown down, the men started growling, and then they were all carted off in different directions.

In order to explain why she was crying, Zoe had to show Dagger both the tattoos. That meant they spent the entire rest of the day in bed, with Dagger showing her his appreciation. He was over the moon after seeing his, and he loved that she got one for her sister as well. Just before they fell asleep for the night, he surprised her by dragging a box out from under his bed. When she opened it, she pulled out a beautiful leather vest. It had her nickname Firecracker on it, and it said Property of Dagger on the back. Of course, then she had to show him her appreciation for the vest, and they didn't end up falling asleep until a lot later. It was a perfect day.

Epilogue

Dagger stood down by the lake. He was wearing jeans, a white tee, his vest, and his boots. He looked no different than he did every day, but he was nervous as fuck. Trike stood at his side, and Preacher stood behind him, but he was completely ignoring them. His eyes were trained on the cabin to his left, as that's the cabin his Firecracker would be coming out of. The trees were once more covered in twinkling lights, but this time they were pink. The lanterns also hung from the trees, and they were painted a soft pink as well. Dagger had to admit it was beautiful.

Dagger couldn't believe he was marrying his girl in just a few minutes. He never thought this day would come. He had actually resigned himself to never meeting his one, figuring he was good on his own. He had liked his life, at least until he had first seen her. She had turned his world upside down, and now he couldn't be happier about that. Zoe and Lion were the best things to happen to him.

Dagger could even put aside the shit his brothers were pulling today. All the asses sat in their seats completely barefoot. They thought this was hilarious. They were grinning like loons, but it didn't bother him. Finally, a song started to play, and Zoe stepped out of the cabin on Lion's arm. She didn't have any parents or siblings, and she had wanted Lion to be a part of the ceremony. This was a big deal for the boy, and he beamed with pride as he escorted her across the lawn.

Of course, the wedding march wasn't what played. Raid had brought out the stupid harp, and the brothers were standing and singing Kumbaya as he played. Dagger tried to ignore them, but finally he had to give in, and a huge grin split across his face. His brothers were fucking funny.

As soon as Zoe got close, Dagger charged down the isle and pulled her from Lion. Then he tipped her back and kissed her. He couldn't help it. Her dress was to die for, her hair was down, and the look on her face took his breath away. Lion just laughed and went to sit beside Wrench. When he was done, he pulled back and looked into her eyes.

"You ready to marry me, Firecracker?" he growled.

"I was born to marry you," Zoe replied with a grin. Then she grabbed his hand, and it was her that dragged him up to Preacher.

The ceremony was quick, and he didn't hear a thing. He said his vows when Preacher prompted him, but the whole time he grinned like a loon and stared at his girl. He was over the moon. Then he was kissing her again, and he couldn't seem to stop. She sagged against him and kissed him back just as passionately. When they pulled back once more, it was to catcalls and whistling from the brothers, and tears from the girls.

When they turned to run down the isle, all the brothers pulled out the water guns. Dagger stood frozen for a minute, then grinned at his new wife and grabbed her hand. She threw back her head and laughed as they dashed through the jets of water, completely uncaring about the water that soaked them. He loved that about her. She embraced life now and smiled all the time. He knew she still missed her sister, but she was doing so much better.

When they reached their cabin, Dagger threw open the door and pulled her inside. As soon as it was shut, he peeled the wet dress off her and threw it to the side. Then he carried her to the bedroom and dropped her on the bed.

"We have a party to go to," she laughed as she swatted at his hands.

"Oh no," Dagger denied. "Those asses soaked you. I have to make sure you're warm and don't get sick."

She laughed. "Oh, you do, do you?"

"Are you happy?" he asked as he covered her body with his.

"I never thought I'd be happy again," she admitted to him. "But you make me happy. You breathe life into me, and you make me want to live. I love you, Damian."

"I love you too, Zoe," he instantly replied.

Dagger and Zoe made it to the party about three hours later, and nobody cared. They drank, they laughed, and they celebrated life. It was a day both would never forget, and the beginning of a long happy life. A life that neither ever expected to have.

About the Author

MEGAN FALL is a mother of three who helps her husband run his construction business. She has been writing all her life, but with a push from her daughter, started publishing. It's the best thing she ever did. When she's not writing, you can find her at the beach. She loves searching for rocks, sea glass, driftwood and fossils. She believes in ghosts, collects ridiculous amounts of plants, and rides on the back of her hubby's motorcycle.

MEGAN FALL

Look for Megan's other books.

STONE KNIGHTS MC SERIES

Finding Ali
Saving Cassie
Loving Misty
Rescuing Tiffany
Guarding Alexandria
Protecting Fable
Surviving November
Sheltering Macy
Defending Zoe
Treasuring Maggie (Coming soon)

DEVILS SOLDIERS MC SERIES

Resisting Diesel
Surviving Hawk (Coming soon)

THE ENFORCER SERIES

The Enforcer
The Enforcers Revenge (Coming soon)

OTHER WORLD SERIES
Elemental Prince (Coming soon)

Treasuring Maggie
Stone Knight's Book 10

Chapter One
Sniper

Sniper twisted the throttle on his Harley and pushed her to her limits. The wind whipped at him, and his adrenaline was pumping. He needed this. Sometimes he missed being in the military. He missed the rush he got from combat, and he missed the feel of the sniper rifle in his hands. He'd sit on a roof with the sand blowing around him and the sun burning through his fatigues for hours. Waiting patiently to get a high priority target in his sights. His patience was tested then, but it was those times when he had to take a shot while avoiding the gunfire all around him, that he missed the most.

Raid had been his spotter, and the brother had become his best friend. Thank god when he got out, Raid followed him here and joined the same MC. It was nice still having him at his back. He glanced in his rear-view mirror, and Raid was right there, pushing his own Harley just as hard as he was. He grinned and took the next corner without letting up at all. Raid grinned back and kept with him. It was a dance just like in the military. The two were completely in sync, knowing each other so well, they could anticipate what the other would do. It had saved their lives on more then one occasion.

Sniper got out for his sister. Misty had been blinded temporarily in a car accident that took their parents lives. Sniper had been allowed to stay for the funeral and get Misty sorted, before he had to return to his post. It was heartbreaking to leave her, but his girl Carly had reassured him that she would take care of her. In the end Carly went bat shit crazy and tried to kill his sister. She would have died if it hadn't been for Trike. The brother had fallen hard for her and had saved her life. She even got her sight back, and Trike had married her and given her a little boy.

But Carly had destroyed Sniper. He had trusted her to keep his baby sister safe, and she had almost cost Misty her life. He'd never forgive himself for putting his faith in the wrong person. Not only that, but it was his girlfriend. The girl he had planned to marry. He'd always wanted a family. He wanted someone to come home to, someone he could love, and someone to carry his child one day. Now all those things were a distant memory, and something he wasn't sure he even wanted anymore. Life sucked sometimes, and he even had thoughts of reenlisting. But his sister was thrilled he was home, and he couldn't hurt her by leaving again.

Sniper saw the gates of the compound coming up, so he was forced to shift down and slow the bike. The gates rolled open, and he took the turn a lot slower as he and Raid pulled through. He headed for the clubhouse, and backed his bike into a spot near the end of the line of Harleys. Raid parked his as well and then dismounted and headed his way.

"You pushed it hard today. You okay?" Raid asked with a slight frown.

"Yep," Sniper immediately replied. "Just one of those days. Had to get the blood pumping."

Raid nodded, and he knew the brother understood. It was hard returning to civilization and everyday life. Some days it just didn't work. The club was fucking fantastic, but sometimes he just needed his space.

"Let's head out back and take a couple shots," Raid suggested. Sniper nodded, thinking that was a great idea.

The club had a range set up in the woods beyond the property. It was well out of the way and completely fenced off. He and Raid were frequent users, taking their sniper rifles and disappearing for hours. It was something that always relaxed him and cleared his head. He knew it did that same thing for Raid.

Something had to give soon though. He couldn't keep riding recklessly and shooting for hours. He needed something else to take his mind off things. Maybe a visit to Diesel's club would get his head straightened out. The men of The Devils Soldiers were all ex-military, and he could talk to them and be completely frank. A lot of them were suffering from similar problems to his.

He pushed through the clubhouse and headed for his room, nodding at the brothers he passed. Once he had his sniper bag slung over his shoulder, and he felt the weight, his body relaxed. He caught up to Raid outside his room, and they headed for the range together. It took about ten minutes to set up and check his weapon, before he was able to take his first shot. He lay on the hard ground, his rifle set comfortably on his shoulder as he waited for Raid. The brother had his laser rangefinder out, and he called coordinates and wind speeds to help Sniper line up his shot. Then he switched to his binoculars as Sniper made adjustments.

"Send it," Raid ordered.

Sniper took a deep breath and squeezed the trigger as he fired. "Call," he ordered back.

"Broke clean," Raid responded as he dropped the binoculars, and Sniper grinned. It was rare he missed, and Raid had just confirmed it was a perfect shot, dead centre.

"Again?" Raid asked, and Sniper just smirked. Raid shook his head and smirked back, as the brothers both set up to take another shot.

Made in United States
North Haven, CT
17 November 2022

26838673R00183